BOOK

THE MALEVOLENT MAGNETISM OF AMERICA'S FAVORITE VAMPIRE—REVEALED FOR THE FIRST TIME IN BOOK FORM!

You'll love to read about the man you love to hate—Barnabas Collins, the 175-year-old vampire who has captured the hearts of the millions who watch him daily on ABC-TV's DARK SHADOWS.

This never-before-told gothic suspense tale about Barnabas' mysterious past is chock-full of chills enough to thrill every reader!

And be sure to watch for another adventure of the mysterious vampire—THE SECRET OF BARNABAS COLLINS.

Hermes Press

Published by Hermes Press, an imprint of
Herman and Geer Communications, Inc.

Daniel Herman, Publisher
Troy Musguire, Production Manager
Eileen Sabrina Herman, Managing Editor
Alissa Fisher, Graphic Design
Kandice Hartner, Senior Editor
Benjamin Beers, Archivist

2100 Wilmington Road
Neshannock, Pennsylvania 16105
(724) 652-0511
www.HermesPress.com; info@hermespress.com

Book design by Eileen Sabrina Herman
First printing, 2020

LCCN applied for: 10 9 8 7 6 5 4 3 2 1 0
ISBN 978-1-61345-207-3
OCR and text editing by H + G Media and Eileen Sabrina Herman
Proof reading by Eileen Sabrina Herman and Ran Case

From Dan, Louise, Sabrina, Jacob, Ruk'us and Noodle for D'zur and Mellow

Acknowledgments: This book would not be possible without the help and encouragement of Jim Pierson and Curtis Holdings

Printed in Canada

BARNABAS COLLINS
by Marilyn Ross

CONTENTS

PROLOGUE

For a long, eerie moment the mournful howl of some distant animal was wafted in on the sudden gust of wind. Victoria Winters was seated before a blazing log fire in the library of Collinwood with an ancient journal spread out on her lap. She lifted her head and listened, a concerned expression on her face. The strong wind of the February night rattled the tall, multi-paned library window again; sleet scraped the glass furtively like skeleton fingers.

Victoria glanced toward the drawn crimson drapes and saw them shift just a trifle. The quick movement of her head was outlined in fantastic shadow against the wall. And when the full force of the wind returned she once more heard the weird animal cry. It was further away now. She sat back with a sigh to stare at the yellow tongues of fire devouring the giant logs Roger had earlier placed in the gray stone fireplace. As the wood burned it created a changing pattern of flames in green, blue and amber. And there was the gray and black ash, the death of the logs.

With a small frown Victoria allowed her eyes to return to the yellowed pages of the journal before her. There was much of death in its account of the Collins family history. The peculiar crabbed handwriting, now faded and brownish, told her many things she had not known about the Collins clan, which dated back to the early 1700's in this tiny Maine seacoast town. As an interested newcomer she had avidly read any family history that came into her hands. And only this afternoon while dusting books, she had found this personal journal, Jonas Collins', stowed away behind some other volumes on a top shelf of the library, apparently forgotten.

From the time of her coming to Collinwood as private teacher to young David Collins she had been obsessed by the belief that she was in reality blood kin to the family. Her ignorance of her origins and her experiences at the orphanage where she'd grown up had encouraged this belief. And now there had been added several years of living at Collinwood and being treated as one of the closely knit group there. Victoria had come to feel it was truly her home and these were really her people. Yet she would never be sure until she found absolute proof; that was why she devoured any information about the Collins family so avidly.

The wind and storm lashed the library window again and screamed around the chimneys that high above streaked up into the dark and angry night. In the fireplace the flames dipped drunkenly for a moment and the partially burned logs stirred and changed formation as though being arranged by a phantom hand. Victoria suddenly felt a distinct chill of fear and blamed it on the strange account she'd been reading in the journal.

Her eyes sought the page again and she read: "It was on this foggy night in May, 1911, that my daughter Greta died. Only now can I bring myself to write about it. Judith, Cousin Barnabas' adopted daughter, had left our house the same night to marry— we never saw her again. It was indeed the beginning of change at Collinwood. For my poor wife, Margaret, who had so valiantly carried the burden of our child's long illness, fell on her death into a delicate mental and physical state herself from which she has at this date never truly recovered.

"My cousin Barnabas Collins, whom I found likable for all his strange ways, also was shattered by these events. He was devoted to Greta and opposed to his daughter's marriage. Immediately following Greta's death he left Collinwood to return to England. His departure was unexpected by any of us and took place after dark one night. We have not had any word from him since."

There was a space at the end of this account and the next notation in his old journal began with the description of a ship's arrival from the West Indies and a listing of her general cargo. For the business of the Collins family at that earlier date had still included shipping. Later the family fish-packing plant had become their primary concern. With a sigh Victoria closed the book with its worn green linen covers and stared into the fire. The flames created a rippled reflection on her pretty face as she sat there thinking of the past.

She was so occupied by her thoughts she did not hear the footsteps entering the book-lined room. And it wasn't until Elizabeth Stoddard, elegant and lovely in a dark dress, came to stand by her chair with a questioning smile that Victoria knew she was no longer alone.

"You've been reading," Elizabeth said. "How fortunate you are able to concentrate in spite of this awful storm."

Victoria held up the journal. "I only found this today. It's fascinating—the journal of Jonas Collins."

Elizabeth raised her shapely eyebrows. "Jonas Collins! He was my grandfather."

Victoria rose and held the book out to her. "This is his journal from 1890 until 1921."

"I haven't seen this in years," Elizabeth said, flipping through the musty pages of the journal.

"I found it back of some other books when I was dusting in here this morning. I wonder if he kept any other journals? Or did he die soon after he completed this one?"

"I'm sure he died in 1937," Elizabeth said, her brow furrowing as she considered. "He was seventy-seven at the time. And my grandmother lived on until 1948. She was eighty-three when she died."

"That would be the Margaret referred to in the journal."

"Grandmother Margaret Collins! How long ago it seems! I was in my first year of college when we lost her."

"Your grandfather had an interesting way of writing," Victoria said. "I feel as if I'd lived here in those old days and really met some of the people."

Elizabeth smiled as she held the book. "I was around nine when he died. I picture him as thin and bent with arthritis. He wore pince-nez with a black silk ribbon attached from them to his lapel. And he used to like to hold me on his knee and tell me stories about his boyhood."

"I'm sure you must have liked them," Victoria said, "judging by the way he holds interest in this journal. I haven't been able to put it aside."

"Good reading for a stormy night."

"What about Barnabas Collins?" Victoria asked. "I've never heard him spoken of before."

"Haven't you? It's a rather special name in our family. The first Barnabas Collins was a son of Joshua who was the original Collins of Collinsport. The one Grandfather refers to was Barnabas Collins, a cousin from England. He came here around the turn of the century."

"And he left in May, 1911, so your grandfather writes." Elizabeth nodded. "That would be about right. Grandmother often told me about him. It appears he was a strange man and very devoted to the girl, Judith, whom he adopted. Her departure seems to have wrecked him. My grandmother claimed it was a dark day for everyone here."

Victoria regarded the older woman with wonder as the storm came to lash at the window once more. "Then you've heard about it all firsthand."

"Yes. As Grandmother grew older, she kept going back to those other days. I can remember her saying that Barnabas Collins was a striking man but fearsome."

"Fearsome?"

"He was something of an eccentric," Elizabeth explained. "Grandmother said he spent all his days at the old house working on some experiments. He was a scientist. But I guess nothing ever came of all his work. He probably gave it up when he went back to England."

Victoria found herself more and more interested. "I'd like to hear your grandmother's version of those days," she said. "What did Barnabas Collins look like?"

Elizabeth smiled thinly. "I can show you."

"Really?"

"Come out to the foyer with me," the older woman said, leading the way.

Victoria followed her to the darkened hall. Elizabeth switched on the overhead light. Standing before a large portrait with a gold frame that Victoria had never paid much attention to, the older woman said, "That is the first Barnabas Collins. And as Grandmother told it, this cousin from England resembled him remarkably."

Victoria stared at the portrait of a stern-faced young man with heavy black hair, strands of which carelessly strayed across a dominant forehead, whose deep-set eyes stared back from under shaggy brows. The high cheekbones gave way to cadaverous hollows; his mouth was thick-lipped and sullen. Not a pleasant face and yet, in a perverse way, a handsome one.

"I've never really looked at him before," Victoria admitted with a tiny shiver. "Would you call it a cruel face?"

"Tormented," Elizabeth said quietly as she stared at the portrait. "That Barnabas knew tragedy also. It was a lost love that drove him from here. And he founded the English branch of the family."

"So long ago!"

"And yet still a part of us today," Elizabeth said. "For surely we're the product of all those past generations." She smiled. "I forgot for a moment you are not one of the family."

"I forget that myself," Victoria confessed. "Having never known a family until I came here, it has been easy to adopt this one."

Elizabeth placed an arm affectionately around her as they turned away from the portrait. "But we do feel you are one of us. That's so true!"

"I'd like to hear more about Barnabas and his adopted daughter Judith and what happened," Victoria said.

"I'll tell you all that Grandmother told me," Elizabeth promised. She turned off the foyer light before they walked slowly back to the library. When they entered the book-lined room again Elizabeth picked one of the logs by the fireplace and with a deft movement tossed it into the fire. "That should burn for a while," she said, smiling at Victoria. "Now let's sit down and make ourselves comfortable."

Victoria sat in the big easy chair and Elizabeth took a wing chair across from her. Victoria asked, "Did your grandmother recall when Barnabas Collins first appeared?"

Elizabeth closed her eyes, remembering. "I believe it was after dusk one night in 1902."

Ghostly fingers of sleet again scraped the window.

CHAPTER 1

The gale that lashed the windows of Collinwood with sleet also brought a swirling cloak of snow to a battered headstone in the Collins private cemetery. In that lonely iron-fenced square of land, mottled with slabs of New England granite to mark the resting places of so many generations of the family, the storm held full sway. But nowhere was it more fierce than around the worn gravestone with the barely readable inscription, "Margaret Collins, 1865-1948."

And as the wind went on howling, a plaintive feminine voice was borne on it. "Ah, yes, dear little Elizabeth, you were only a child when I told you about Barnabas and those dark days. Therefore I spared you the full horror of the real truth—the secret of Barnabas that I have carried with me to my grave! The secret that only I was to discover!"

Margaret Collins always found the days a little too short. At thirty-seven she was the mistress of Collinwood, a mansion which was the wonder of the county with its forty-odd rooms, all of which demanded her care. Her husband, Jonas, only a few years older than herself, was fully thirty years older in manner. She felt she understood why and sympathized with him.

He had been forced to assume the responsibility for the Collins Shipping Company at a fairly early age. It had matured him beyond his years. The day of the sailing ship was over; he was having a battle to make the line pay. Their marriage had brought him a brief span of happiness, followed by the birth of a daughter whose legs were so badly deformed that she was doomed to spend all her days in a wheelchair. He had retreated into a cold, aloof shell, concentrating on his work. He delegated the details of running the great mansion to Margaret.

She was still a Titian-haired beauty, full of figure and with a charming smile. She was a deeply religious woman and devoted to her invalid daughter, Greta, a golden-haired replica of herself as far as most people could tell, for Margaret allowed no one to see the distorted limbs which were always covered by a blanket as she sat in her wheelchair.

The doctors in Portland and Boston who had viewed Greta's deformity had pronounced the twisted, abnormally thin limbs beyond any hope of being cured. Yet there was no sadness in the afflicted girl and Margaret had pretended to feel none either.

They had accepted Greta's affliction as a normal consequence of a life in which many were stricken in one way or another. Margaret educated the girl herself, delighted to find she had a lively, intelligent mind to match her beauty of face. And Margaret had the solace of her son, now away studying in Boston.

To ease the strained financial plight they found themselves in, Margaret attempted to take care of the big house with a minimum of help. Two young village girls, Ada and Patience Griffin, sisters in their late teens, acted as maids and did general housework. They were given to giggling and were inclined to pay too much attention to the many swains from the village who came to escort them to town on their free days. There was also Granny Entwhistle, who had been the housekeeper in her day, and still remained on though close to ninety, addled and given to hearing spirit voices. And as handyman and servant to wheel Greta's chair on her excursions outdoors there was the simple-minded, oversized Luke Sinnot.

Luke was an awkward, hulking youth of twenty-odd, possessed of a warm heart and a doglike devotion toward the seventeen-year-old Greta. Margaret had welcomed him when he'd been refused employment in the village. People in Collinsport had a backward attitude toward the retarded and refused to see Luke's worth as an individual and his potential usefulness. Some even declared that he should be confined to a madhouse.

Margaret, however, had no qualms in hiring him, though her husband had several times irritably suggested she was making a mistake. Jonas had warned her, "There is no telling when Luke may change for the worse. He is a maniac and I don't think we should trust our daughter in his charge."

Margaret had faced up to her husband in this as she'd had to in so many other things. "Luke is gentle and kind. As for being dangerous to Greta, he worships her and I have no worries concerning him."

So that settled that—at least for a while, in an uneasy household where things seldom remained settled long. On this particular June evening Margaret was feeling a pleasant, relaxed weariness. Greta had been safely installed in her downstairs bedroom next to the library. Jonas had gone back to the shipping office down by the docks to work. And Margaret, having completed the bottling of many batches of strawberry jam with the vague assistance of old Granny Entwhistle, decided she would take a walk along the cliffs high above the ocean.

She was wearing a dark print cotton dress with a white lace collar and jabot. Going to the closet off the hall she selected a light shawl and placed it around her shoulders. Maine nights could be cool even in late June. Then she started out on her walk. Margaret rather liked being alone. She had the nature of a mystic. And she felt very close to the old estate with all its secrets and mysteries. As she slowly made her way across the open lawn to the path that fringed the cliffs she was filled with a kind of peace.

Dusk sheathed the countryside in a dull blue haze. Seagulls circled around overhead uttering their melancholy night calls. Far down the bay she could see the first faint regular beam of the Collins Point lighthouse. She smiled to herself as she thought how the Collins imprint was on everything in the area. She had married into an important family.

And it had once been a wealthy one. Jonas vowed it would be again; it was for this goal he slaved both day and night, while she did the best she could with a quarter of the help the house had once regularly employed. They had even rented the older house that dated back to the early 1700 to make ends meet. But the elderly schoolteacher and his daughter who had lived there for almost a year had returned to Boston. So now the house was empty again and bringing in no revenue although Jonas had told her he was seeking a new tenant.

She sighed. Somehow they would manage. And then interrupting her thoughts of these mundane problems and bringing her to a halt was the unexpected feeling of nearby danger. It had come to her with stunning swiftness and pressed against her heart so tightly she was shocked. Never had she felt unsafe on the grounds before. It was as if unseen eyes were studying her malevolently, appraising her weakness with derision. With an automatic gesture she pulled the shawl tightly about her shoulders and was alarmed to find herself trembling.

Was she being followed? Could this be a sixth sense warning her? She looked fearfully behind but saw no one. Was it some kind of illness taking hold of her after her hard-working day in the heat? She didn't understand but she felt she should turn and go back to the house at once. And then she rebelled. She had never been a creature of whims or caprices. She wouldn't be now.

A determined expression crossed her attractive face and she walked on with head held high. Then, as she neared the turn in the path near the cliff's highest point, she saw the caped figure standing staring down at the rocky shore a hundred feet or more of a sheer drop below. She slowed her step, her eyes straining against the gathering dusk, amazed to find a stranger at this lonely spot.

The pound of the incoming waves came loud in her ears. Her heart was beating rapidly as she wavered between fear and excitement. As she drew closer to the man in the dark caped coat she saw that he wore no hat, but carried a black cane with a silver handle. His back was to her but now he turned very slowly and stood there staring at her with great intentness.

Margaret Collins could almost feel the power of those deep-set eyes as they fixed upon her. The melancholy, almost cadaverous face with its high cheekbones, and the thick black hair in disarray across the intelligent forehead were strange to her, and yet familiar. She couldn't understand it. Nor could she explain why she had come to a full stop a few feet distant from him.

The stranger's rich voice carried a British accent. "You are Mrs. Margaret Collins, I'm sure."

She found her voice. "Yes. How did you know?"

He smiled, revealing glistening white teeth, and she began to see that the stern face had a certain charm. He said, "Your husband described you to me when I talked with him at his office a short time ago."

"Oh, you have met Mr. Collins!" She was surprised; her husband hadn't mentioned any stranger.

He nodded. "Yes. I have just come from his office. My man and myself. May I introduce myself? I am Barnabas Collins—a cousin of your husband's from England."

He held out his hand and she stepped forward to take it in an almost mechanical fashion. Her eyes fixed on his, she said in a low voice, "Welcome to Collinwood, Cousin Barnabas."

"Thank you, Cousin Margaret," he said suavely. She felt the power of his handgrip and was puzzled that at the same time his flesh should feel so icy cold.

Barnabas held her hand in his a trifle longer than might have been necessary. But when he released it he turned to stare down at the rocks below. "It hasn't changed at all," he said. "Still the sad setting for the widow's wail and the appearance of the Phantom Mariner."

Margaret's eyebrows raised. "You know all our legends. You have been here before?"

He looked suddenly uneasy. "I'm sorry, I was carried away. I have never been here. But I have heard the place described so often by my late grandfather."

She stared at the man in the caped coat. "But of course; now I know why you seemed to have such a familiar look. You are a descendant of the first Barnabas Collins, the one who left here for England a century ago. And I must say you bear an uncanny resemblance to him."

He smiled again to reveal the long gleaming teeth. "Really? You do think so? I'm pleased that I should resemble Great-Grandfather Barnabas. He was rather a pleasant man."

"A handsome one in his own fashion," she said impulsively. "And so are you," she finished in blushing confusion.

Barnabas appeared pleased. "Thank you," he said. "It is good to find my cousin with such a delightful wife. I'm certain we shall be friends."

"I'm sure we shall," she said. "Of course Jonas invited you to stay with us."

The tall, dark man inclined his head. "Indeed he did," he said. "But at my request we came to another arrangement. I plan to be here some time and I'm working on some rather unusual experiments. I need space and privacy. So I have prevailed on Jonas to rent me the old house. In fact, at this very moment my servant Hare is there moving in my things and making preparations for the night."

Margaret was confused by the speed with which all this had been agreed upon. But she supposed Jonas had jumped at the opportunity of rental since he was anxious for the revenue from it. "If that is what you want, Cousin Barnabas. But you must dine with us while you are here. And often."

"Thank you, my dear," he said urbanely. "But do not be offended if you see little of me. I'm rarely abroad during the day. It is dining the daylight hours that I must give my full time to my scientific explorations. And I'm a person with an extremely light appetite. My taste in nourishment is somewhat peculiar. So you must bear with me."

Margaret had begun to sense a similarity between Jonas and this cousin. They both were aloof and cold, both devoured with an unrelenting ambition. She said, "We would not wish to intrude on you. But you are one of the family and the freedom of our house is yours. You must visit us often."

"That I promise to do," Barnabas said. "I hear you have two grown children. A son in Boston and your daughter at home."

"Yes," Margaret said, a touch of regret coming into her tone. "No doubt Jonas told you Greta is confined to a wheelchair. But she is a lovely, intelligent child. I know you'll enjoy meeting her."

"I look forward to it," Barnabas said with great sincerity. "I do not think she should feel herself cut off in any way because of her affliction. Are we not all deformed in either soul or body, even if it is not immediately apparent? There are no perfect beings."

She felt herself losing some of her awe and warming to the stranger.

"Thank you for saying that," she said. "I wish you could express the same sentiment to my husband. Jonas is so bitter about Greta's affliction."

"I must speak to him on that subject." He took her arm to stroll back toward the house with her amid the gathering darkness. She noticed now that the cane he carried had a silver wolf's head.

She was losing some of her feelings of fear and yet she was not at ease with him. She said, "Only my husband, my daughter and I are here, except for a few servants."

Barnabas nodded. "A nice family group. By the way, my man Hare is rather a frightening looking chap—large and burly, with a rather ugly face. And he happens to be deaf and dumb. But he is devoted and quite mild in temperament. So do not be alarmed by him."

She promised she wouldn't and went on to tell him about Luke Sinnot and the retarded young man's devotion to Greta. She also mentioned Granny Entwhistle and the two servant girls. By this time he was standing at the door with her.

It was dark. He glanced out across the ocean. "There is little moon tonight," he said. "It is a dark homecoming for me."

"Homecoming?" she said. "But your home is England."

He responded with a low laugh. "I spoke of it in the sense of a Collins returning to the ancestral home. I imagine by this time Hare has my bed prepared and most of our things safely installed."

"If you need linen or anything of the sort, do come back and get it."

"Indeed I will," he promised. And with a smile and a bow he kissed her hand. She almost drew it back with a start for the touch of his lips had been as icy and chilling as the feel of his hand.

He said goodnight again and walked off briskly toward the old house which was located in the field beyond the outbuildings. She watched his retreating figure merge with the shadows and realized she was trembling again.

It was her bedtime. She left a candle burning in the foyer

for Jonas when he returned. And for a moment she stood there studying the portrait of the first Barnabas Collins in the flickering candlelight. There was no question that the man she had just met bore a startling resemblance to the one whose portrait had been painted so many years ago.

She made her way upstairs to her bedroom. For some time now she and Jonas had slept in adjoining rooms and for long periods the door between them was never opened.

By the time she had extinguished the lamp and slid between the sheets there was a pale gleam of moonlight. She closed her eyes and tried to rest but she still was haunted by the stern features of Cousin Barnabas and those powerful eyes.

Then there came the soft bump against her window. It was repeated again and after a short pause it came once more. Curious, she raised herself on an elbow and stared toward the window whose drapes she had not closed. And what she saw made her give vent to a scream of sheer terror. An enormous bat was beating against the window. She watched with the fascination of horror as it came close again and there was the crash of breaking glass and the bat came hovering into the room directly above her. She smelled its dank odor and felt its soft, slippery wings. Hurling herself across the bed away from it, she cried out for help.

CHAPTER 2

Margaret fought the vile attacking creature off with her fists as its wings sought to envelop her. She continued to scream, not even aware she was doing it, in a fear such as she'd never experienced before. Then the door from the adjoining room opened.

"What is it?" It was Jonas speaking.

Before she could reply there was a frantic rustle of wings and the bat left her. She sat up gasping and weeping as Jonas came across the shadowed room to her. Grasping her by the shoulders, he stared down at her sternly.

"What is the cause of your hysterics?" he demanded.

"The bat!" she pointed to the window, still weeping. "It broke the glass and forced its way in. It was hideous!"

"A bat large enough to break the window!" Jonas sounded incredulous.

"Look for yourself," she said.

"I will." He went over to examine the window. After a moment he turned from it. "It is broken," he admitted. "But surely it must have happened some other way."

"I tell you it was a monstrous bat! It came in here and attacked me!" Margaret insisted tearfully.

"It certainly had vanished by the time I came in," Jonas said.

"It seemed to go at the sound of your voice."

Her husband advanced slowly across to her bed again. "You realize this is a most incredible story?"

"I can't help it. It's true!"

"You've had a bad dream."

"No."

He stood there in the shadows frowning. "You must put the episode out of your mind and try to get to sleep."

Margaret tensed. "I'll not be able to sleep. I'm too terrified. With that window as it is, the bat will force its way in again."

"I'll draw the drapes."

As he started back to his own room she called to him, "Please! Leave the door open."

He hesitated with his hand on the doorknob as if considering. At last, in a grudging tone, he agreed, "Very well. If you wish it. Goodnight."

The knowledge that he could be summoned easily helped quiet her nerves. At last she fell into a deep sleep, disturbed only toward dawn by eerie dreams of Cousin Barnabas coming toward her, his arms raised so that the cape of his black coat spread to give him a batlike appearance. With a strangled cry of horror she woke herself up.

But she was alone in the room. And through the doorway she could hear the sound of her husband's regular breathing as he slept. She lay back trembling and wet with perspiration. Of course it had been a nightmare. But why should she have mixed Barnabas up in it? Perhaps because the meeting with him was still so fresh in her mind. And because he was such a dominating personality. Dawn was creeping in around the drapes. She closed her eyes for another short period of sleep.

At the breakfast table that morning she questioned Jonas about the newcomer. "It all seems to have been arranged so quickly," she said.

Jonas gave her an icy glance. "Would you have me turn my cousin away?"

"No. Especially not when he is so willing to pay rent for the old house."

Her husband frowned. "That is the way he wanted it. And I may say it suits me very well."

"It is our duty to show him some hospitality," Margaret insisted. "I'm sure he'll be anxious to meet a few of the townsfolk. We should hold some kind of party for him."

"We have no money for that sort of nonsense," her husband said angrily. "And in any event, Cousin Barnabas has made it clear he wants a deal of privacy."

She had not expected him to agree. But she still secretly hoped that she might somehow later manage a modest affair from the housekeeping funds to introduce this cousin from England to the people of Collinsport. When she went to Greta's bedroom to help her dress, she found her daughter had already learned about Barnabas.

"Patience told me," she said as she sat on the edge of the bed in her long silk nightgown.

Margaret pretended amusement. "And how did that pretty little maid of ours come to make his acquaintance?"

A mischievous smile crossed her blonde daughter's lovely face. "Patience had her boyfriend out here to see her. She walked as far as the gate with him. On the way back she suddenly became frightened of the darkness. She began to run and stumbled. Strong hands picked her up and they belonged to Cousin Barnabas. He talked to her a few minutes. She doesn't seem to be able to remember what he said, she was so flustered. But she thinks he's wonderful."

"Indeed," Margaret said, catering to her daughter's mood as she nearly always did. "Then we have the maid's opinion of him."

Later, when Greta was fully dressed and wheeled out in her chair to have breakfast, she asked, "How soon can I meet Cousin Barnabas?"

Her mother smiled at her. "You'll have to restrain your curiosity. Barnabas will not be seeing us during the day. He is engaged at the old house. He is doing some important experiments."

Greta looked disappointed. "Then I won't be able to talk to him until this evening?"

"I'm afraid not," she said. But secretly she was glad of this. She still hadn't made up her mind about the man from England— she wasn't sure whether she wanted him around her daughter or not.

Greta was filled with a young girl's eager questions. "What does he look like? I'm sure he must be handsome to impress Patience so! And is he charming?"

Her mother gave her a tolerant smile. Greta was at an age when most young women were having their first romances. It had been her crippled daughter's lot to enjoy young love only at second hand. And this seemed such a shame since Greta was a beauty otherwise. No wonder the arrival of this cousin from England had so excited her.

"He is an impressive looking man," Margaret told her. "And charming as well. And you'll meet him in tune. But we must allow him the privacy he needs for his work."

"What sort of work?"

Margaret sighed. "He really didn't explain. But if you want an idea of what he looks like you'll find he bears a remarkable resemblance to the first Barnabas Collins, his ancestor, whose portrait is in the foyer."

"Really?" Greta seemed thrilled. "I must take a look at it after breakfast."

And she did. Margaret wheeled her out and they lingered by the portrait for some time. Greta commented on the brooding strength of the somber features of the first Barnabas and was more anxious than ever to meet his great-grandson.

They were still in the foyer when Luke Sinnot came in awkwardly in his work clothes and touched a hand to his forelock. "Will Miss Greta want her trip outdoors now, ma'am?" he asked.

Margaret smiled at the big man with his blank childish features in contrast to the dark stubble of beard that showed him to be an adult. Turning to Greta, she asked, "Do you wish Luke to take you now?"

"Yes. I do. It's nice out and the sun will warm me," Greta said. She smiled at Luke. "Today will you take me by the old house?"

Luke nodded. "The old house," he repeated in his slow way.

"Mind," Margaret warned them as Luke started to wheel the girl to the front door, "you're not to disturb Cousin Barnabas."

As Luke left the wheelchair to open the door, Greta smiled back at her mother mischievously. "Of course I'll not bother him," she said. "But if he should happen to be anywhere outdoors I will introduce myself."

Margaret watched the door close after her with a feeling of uneasiness. It was hard to explain the sudden mood of apprehension that had come to her. She tried to shrug it off as her natural concern for her daughter. She was worried that in her eagerness Greta might intrude on the stern Barnabas and receive less of a greeting than she expected. It boiled down to the fact she was afraid that her daughter's feelings might be hurt.

With a sigh she went back upstairs. Ada, the older and more sedate of the two maids, was already working on the beds. Margaret paused to tell her to clean the glass up where the window had been broken in her room. And she added that Luke would have to repair the window before night. There was extra glass in the shed out back of the house. Before going back downstairs Margaret went into her room and studied the pane that had been broken. Only a few jagged fragments of glass remained held by the putty. It was clear the bat must have used great force to shatter it.

She shuddered in remembrance and quickly left the room. Downstairs she found the other maid, Patience, busy in the kitchen and old Granny Entwhistle nodding by an empty tea cup at the end of the big kitchen table.

Margaret crossed to Patience first. "I hear you had an adventure last night."

The pretty little brown-haired maid paused in washing the dishes to turn to her with a smile. "Yes, ma'am."

"You met Mr. Barnabas Collins, our cousin recently arrived from England."

"I did, ma'am."

"I understand you fell and he helped you."

"Yes, ma'am," Patience said. "He is a very kind gentleman."

"I'm glad you have such a good opinion of him," Margaret said. And then she noticed the maid had a neat white linen handkerchief pinned around her throat. "Why are you wearing that?" she asked.

Patience looked embarrassed. Her hand automatically went up to touch the neat bandage. "I have chafe marks on my throat," she said. "It must have happened when I fell."

"Oh!" Margaret said. "I trust they are of no consequence."

"No. I'm sure they'll heal in a day or two."

"Let me know if they give you any trouble," Margaret told her. And then she went over to where Granny Entwhistle sat dozing by the table.

On her approach the old woman looked up with a concerned expression on her pinched face. She had thin white hair drawn straight back and gathered in a knot at the nape of her neck. She had been a small woman and was now completely dried up.

"A bird of ill omen!" she announced solemnly with a smacking of her toothless gums as Margaret came to stand by her.

"What is it now, Granny?" Margaret wanted to know. She was familiar with the old woman's complaints and prophecies of doom.

A scrawny hand reached for the empty tea cup and held it up for her to see. "In the tea leaves," the old woman said. "A black bird of evil over this house."

Magaret's first reaction was mild amusement and then her brow furrowed as she looked into the cup held by the trembling hand. For clearly outlined in the tea leaves was the shape of a bat.

She took the cup from the old woman's hand and stared into it. "It looks more like a bat than a bird, Granny."

"The shadow of darkness has come over Collinwood again," Granny said with a wise nod. "But then, no one listens to me anymore."

"Of course we listen to you, Granny," Margaret consoled her as she returned the cup to the saucer on the table. But she knew the old woman's lament was true. They were all much too involved with their daily problems to pay much attention to the old woman.

Greta came back from her excursion around the grounds in a subdued mood. She told her mother, "The house could be deserted if you didn't know better. Not a sign of anyone there."

"I warned you," Margaret reminded her. "Cousin Barnabas said he would be remaining inside and keep strictly to himself all during the day."

But when late afternoon arrived she went to the kitchen and had one of the maids prepare her a basket with fresh dinner rolls, butter and some cakes. And she walked through the yard and past the barns to the original Collins house that was now known as the old house. The sun was still bright and it was pleasantly warm.

Knowing how stiff Jonas could be, she was anxious to make Barnabas Collins feel as welcome as she could. She hoped this bit of homemade cooking would please him and wondered how he would fare for food. No doubt the servant, Hare, whom he'd spoken of, was trained in that department.

The shutters at all the front windows remained closed, as if no one had taken up residence there. It struck her that Barnabas must prefer shadowed rooms—something to do with his experiments, perhaps. She knocked on the weatherbeaten oak door loudly enough to be heard inside. She waited; the perpetual wind from the ocean sighed through the elm shade trees surrounding the old house. And somehow this communicated a fresh feeling of uneasiness in her. She knocked again.

A moment later there was the pound of unsteady footsteps coming toward the door. And all at once it was thrown open and a purple angry face peered out at her from the dark hall. She almost gasped at the shock of his ugliness. He was short, squat and his features had an apelike cast. Also he was hairy! His heavy black hair came far down on his slanting forehead and his chin showed a stubble of bluish beard. The smell of whiskey on his breath was strong even a distance from him. His malevolent, bloodshot eyes regarded her with utter hostility. And the thick lips curled to give out with a guttural warning. The grunting sound reminded her that he was deaf and dumb.

Summoning a forced smile, she offered him the basket.

With a gesture of rejection he pushed it away and growled again. And then he slammed the door in her face and she heard his footsteps retreating to the rear of the house. She stood there in consternation for a moment. Her friendly overture had not gotten far.

Defeated, she turned and walked back to Collinwood. Why would Barnabas Collins, who seemed a cultured gentleman, employ such a person? Surely a servant like Hare would continually involve him in trouble and explanations! It was hard to understand. But then it was all puzzling. There was an air of mystery about Barnabas she would like to have explained.

Her husband, Jonas, was not the one to do it. At dinner that evening she tried to sound him out about Barnabas and the ancestor who had left the estate long ago to settle in England. But Jonas was reluctant to give her anything but the most casual explanation.

"Barnabas was a son of Joshua Collins," her husband said. "He went to England around eighteen-hundred and was never heard of again."

"Is that the whole story?" Margaret had asked.

Jonas gave her one of his icy glances. "What more could there be? Don't expect a romantic scandal attached to every family happening."

Greta had smiled covertly at her mother. "Do you think he will visit us tonight?"

"I do not know," Margaret said truthfully. She turned to Jonas. "Will you remain to entertain him in case he should pay us a call?"

Her husband touched a napkin to his lips. "No. I have extra work at the office. We have a sailing in the morning. I must complete the ship's papers."

Greta begged her mother to allow her to remain up later than usual, in case Barnabas should decide to come by. They moved into the big living room with its rich furniture of British pattern and the family portraits on its walnut-paneled walls.

As dusk approached and still there was no sign of the cousin from England Greta requested, "Light the candles in here rather than the lamps. It is so much more romantic. And I want everything to be at its best if Cousin Barnabas comes."

Margaret consented, and with a lighted taper in her hand she moved from table to sideboard from one end of the big room to the other until all the candles were lit. Then she turned to smile at her daughter. "Now are you satisfied?"

From her wheelchair Greta smiled back at her. "It's like an enchanted room. I wish you would never use anything but candles in here."

Margaret was touched by the pleasure the small effort had given her invalid child. And studying her in the soft glow of the candlelight she was again struck by her beauty. What a pity that fate had decreed she would spend all her life in a wheelchair! Her thoughts were interrupted by the sharp summons of the front doorbell.

"That has to be him!" Greta exulted.

And it was. Margaret opened the door and the handsome man with the caped coat was standing there. The deep-set eyes bored into her and his heavy lips parted in a smile to reveal the prominent white teeth she had noticed the previous night.

"The moon seems to have risen earlier tonight," he said, partly turning to indicate the full moon over the ocean in the background. "I trust you do not mind my visiting you."

"Not at all," she said in a quiet voice. "My daughter will be happy to meet you. In fact, she has remained up beyond her usual bedtime for that purpose."

Barnabas raised his heavy eyebrows. "How nice of her." He stepped inside. And as she closed the door, he said, "May I apologize for the stupid behavior of Hare this afternoon. I fear he was drinking when you arrived."

"I had a basket of food for you," she told him. "I'm only sorry he wouldn't accept it."

"It was rude of him," Barnabas agreed. "But to be completely fair, I had given him strict orders I was not to be disturbed. And we have all the food we can possibly use. I laid in a good supply in the village. Hare, in spite of his forbidding appearance, is an excellent cook."

"I felt that might be the explanation," she agreed. "His being deaf and dumb makes it difficult to reach him."

"That is a problem," he confessed. "And yet he is so ideal in other ways I would hesitate to part with him."

"I understand," she said. "May I take your coat?"

Barnabas looked taken back. "No. If you do not mind. I happen to be very cold-blooded. Even at this time of the year I am subject to chills. I shall be more comfortable in it."

She considered this odd but made no comment. She merely said, "Now, do come and meet Greta."

He followed her into the candlelit living room and when he first saw Greta he stopped stock-still. Then he advanced as if in a trance to her wheelchair and knelt on one knee before it as he took her hand and kissed it. He allowed his lips to linger on her hand for a long moment before rising.

Greta's lovely face had crimsoned and she smiled up at

him shyly. "What a truly wonderful greeting, Cousin Barnabas. Welcome to Collinwood."

"I am happy to be here," he said in his sonorous voice. "Especially now that I have met you." His eyes were fixed on her in his peculiarly intent fashion.

Margaret, standing in the background, could see that Greta was enthralled. She felt happy for her daughter and yet wary—afraid she might be hurt.

Stepping forward quickly, she smiled and asked Greta, "Don't you think Cousin Barnabas is the exact image of the portrait in the foyer?"

"I do," Greta agreed happily. And then, shyly, "Except that he is much more handsome than any old portrait."

Barnabas smiled.

"That is a kind exaggeration." Margaret continued, "We have always felt that Greta herself somewhat resembles one of the truly ancient family portraits. The dark one above the sideboard."

Barnabas nodded and without a word went over to the sideboard and stared up at the portrait, a strained expression on his face. Finally he murmured softly, "Josette!"

Margaret had come up close to him. "Josette?" she repeated after him in a questioning tone.

Barnabas' hypnotic eyes met hers. There was an expression of infinite sadness on the gaunt, good-looking face. "But surely you know about Josette?"

"I'm afraid not," Margaret confessed. "I know the family history as far back as a half-century. After that there are many blanks. My husband talks little about his people. He is a silent type of man."

"Josette was engaged to marry Barnabas Collins," the young man from England said solemnly.

"Indeed! Your great-grandfather! But the marriage didn't take place?"

Barnabas shook his head. "No. She killed herself. Threw herself over the cliff."

"Oh, no!" Margaret was caught up in the ancient tragedy by the bleakness in the stranger's tone.

From her wheelchair Greta said, "What an unhappy story, Cousin Barnabas. But I'm not surprised. I've always felt there was a tragic look in her eyes."

Barnabas nodded and turned once again to study the portrait. He made an imposing picture as he stood there highlighted by the flickering of the tall candles at either end of the sideboard. Then with a sigh he left the portrait and crossed to the wheelchair once more.

With a grave smile, he said, "But there is a happy ending to the story. Josette lives again in you. You are very much like her."

Greta's lovely face shadowed and she indicated the blanket covering her malformed limbs. "A flawed reproduction, I fear."

Margaret felt her throat tighten. Coming up beside her daughter, she touched a hand to her shoulder. "You mustn't say such things!"

"Indeed not!" Barnabas exclaimed with one of his rare smiles. "You feel this way because you have been kept here alone too long. You should have gone into the world. You would attract young men galore! A wheelchair wouldn't stop them. Elizabeth Barrett was an invalid and she married Robert Browning, one of the most handsome and talented poets in England."

Greta's face at once brightened. "You are wonderful. Cousin Barnabas. I have never heard anyone talk like you before."

Margaret was once again troubled. What Barnabas had said was quite true: Greta was lovely enough to win any fine man, given the chance. Such a man would overlook her unfortunate deformity. But what a gamble was involved. She had never dared risk her daughter's happiness by exposing her to a world that might or might not reject her according to a whim. She said, "Greta has had frail health. We have tried to protect her."

"Too much, I fear," Barnabas said with that impressive sweeping power of his. "You and her father have done her a wrong. I hope I may be able to help correct it." He smiled at Greta. "I shall tell you about my life in England and try to make you understand why a wheelchair should not stop you from adventuring out into the wide world."

Greta was staring up at him with an absolutely idolizing look. "Do tell me about what it's like to really live in the world, Cousin Barnabas."

Margaret said, "But that must surely be postponed for another evening. It is now time for you to go to bed. Past time!"

"I'm not a child any longer," Greta said petulantly. "It won't do me any harm to stay up a little longer."

Barnabas Collins took one of her hands in his. Looking at Margaret, he said, "I think you should be generous with this lovely girl. Allow me to take a short walk with her in the moonlight before she retires. I'm very well acquainted with manipulating a wheelchair. I had a friend who was confined to one."

"Please, let us go out awhile," Greta begged him. "I have never been in the garden under the moonlight."

He squeezed her hand and then with a commanding air took the wheelchair by the back and swung it around. He told

Margaret, "We shan't stay long. Just a few minutes to enjoy the magic of the night." And he began wheeling her out.

Margaret stood there in the candlelit room staring after them in utter astonishment. It had all happened so quickly she'd not been able to make a proper protest. Now it was too late. To interfere at this moment would mean offending their young English cousin and making Greta unhappy. She listened to the murmur of their voices in the foyer and then Greta's delighted laughter just before the heavy front door closed after them.

Jonas would not approve. But surely there could be no harm in it. And Cousin Barnabas did have a generous amount of charm. He had brought Greta great happiness in a few minutes. And Margaret found herself somewhat convinced by his words that her beloved daughter might yet one day find a truly worthwhile life. She moved quickly to the window to look out and see the two in the garden.

She glimpsed the dark cape swinging from Barnabas' broad shoulders as he wheeled Greta through the garden in the direction of the cliffs. She wondered briefly if she should follow them. No, this would only humiliate Greta and make her feel she was being treated like a child. Better to wait. And yet she was uneasy.

The minutes passed and soon it had been a full quarter-hour since they left. Margaret really began to be concerned. She had not exaggerated in saying Greta's health was fragile, and so long an exposure to the night air wouldn't be good for her lungs. Alarmed at the thought, she went to the front door and opened it wide to follow the two.

As she did so she glanced up at the full moon which was providing a silvery touch to all around her and saw something that made her heart skip a beat. Her hand flew to her breast as she stared at the shadow against the moon. For the shadow was like the outline of a bat!

It brought all last night's horror back to her. She was about to scream her daughter's name when the movement of the wheelchair over the gravel came to her ears. In the next moment Barnabas appeared, wheeling her daughter.

Margaret stepped back as he manipulated the chair easily up the steps and inside. She said, "I was beginning to wonder what was keeping you."

Barnabas smiled. "Greta was enchanted by the night. I did not wish to hurry her. Now I will go. I know it is late."

Greta stretched a hand out to him and her lovely eyes showed a light that was little short of adoration. "Goodnight, Cousin Barnabas," she said softly.

The gaunt man offered her a gentle smile and kissed her hand again. "Goodnight, my dear," he said. "I shall see you tomorrow night."

In spite of his great kindness to her daughter Margaret drew a sigh of relief as she closed the door behind him. She then began wheeling Greta toward her bedroom. "Cousin Barnabas is a strange man," she commented.

"I think he is wonderful," Greta said happily.

As Margaret assisted her daughter into bed, Greta seemed much weaker than usual. "The excitement has been too much for you," she scolded lightly as she pulled the sheets up over her.

Greta's pretty face was radiant as she gazed up at her. "I don't care! Not if I die before morning! This was the most wonderful night of my life."

Margaret felt a chill of fear creep through her. "You mustn't say such things. You mustn't count on Cousin Barnabas so. He will only be here a little while."

"I hope he has come to stay forever," Greta said, seeming in a happy trance.

And it was only then that Margaret noticed the two faintly crimson spots on her daughter's throat . . . marks like tiny wounds!

CHAPTER 3

S taring at the ugly little red marks on her daughter's throat, Margaret said, "There are tiny wounds on your neck as if you'd been bitten!"

Greta gazed up at her absently and touched her fingers to the swollen red spots on her neck. "Perhaps a mosquito or some other night insect."

"Didn't you notice when it happened?" Margaret asked.

"I can't remember being bothered," her daughter said. "Why make such a fuss about it? It's nothing!"

Margaret frowned. "At least you should have some cologne on the spots." She went to the dresser to get the cologne bottle and a handkerchief to apply it.

Afterward she forgot all about the marks. And when she helped Greta dress the next morning she noticed they had vanished. Greta was still thrilled by her meeting with Cousin Barnabas the previous night and talked about him a great deal.

Margaret wheeled her daughter out into the garden to enjoy the morning air and sunshine. They both sat in the shelter of the ornate octagonal summer house which was open at the sides except for the support posts that carried its red shingled roof. Luke had constructed a wooden ramp over the steps leading to the floor of the summer house and so there was no difficulty getting the wheelchair in and out of it.

For a while they sat in lazy silence, Margaret busying herself with some embroidery and Greta staring pensively out at the shimmering blue of the ocean under the sun. Then Greta suddenly said, "Mother, I'd like to know more about Josette."

Margaret, only half-listening, glanced up from her needlework. "Josette?"

"Yes," her daughter said with a hint of reproach in her tone. "You must know who I mean. The girl in that portrait. The one I'm supposed to look like."

Margaret nodded. "Oh, yes."

"There must be some information in the house about her," Greta insisted. "Surely you could search among the old papers in the attic and see if there aren't some of her letters still there. Or at least some mention of her in other people's diaries or letters."

She smiled wanly. "It has been ages since I've tackled those musty old rooms. I think everything of value has been found and brought down to the library. But I've never seen any reference to this Josette. Perhaps your father may be able to help."

The lovely face across from her shadowed. "Father! He won't be interested!"

Margaret knew she was right. So she said, "I promise I'll take a look the first chance I get."

Greta leaned forward eagerly in her wheelchair. "Oh, I wish you would, Mother. I'd so like to surprise Cousin Barnabas with my knowledge of this Josette. I'm sure he knows something of her history and this is his first visit to the house. It's shameful that we have taken so little interest in our past."

She was rather pleased at this sudden display of concern about family history on her daughter's part. Greta had not shown much interest in anything up until now. How good it was that Cousin Barnabas had roused her from her apathy—if only Greta would not become too enamored of this strange young man who could at the best only be with them a brief time. She was about to say this when her daughter spoke again.

"Barnabas is really a very distant relative of mine, isn't he?" she asked her mother plaintively.

Caught by surprise, Margaret smiled and said, "That is true. But it seems gracious that even a distant relative should be called cousin. Don't you agree?"

"Of course I do!" Greta said impulsively. And then with a fetching look of shyness on her pretty face, she added, "But it would not be considered wrong for such distant cousins to marry, would it?"

Margaret was caught off balance. She stared at the pathetic

figure in the wheelchair for a long moment before she answered. She knew she should warn Greta at once to put such notions out of her head, that Barnabas was merely showing an older man's kindness to her because of her affliction. And not to make something romantic of it when this wasn't the case at all.

But Greta looked so happy. The delicate tinge of rose that had come to her cheeks was such a rarity and the shy smile of content so touching Margaret found it impossible to shatter her daughter's dream. She racked her mind to find the proper words.

And she settled for, "Distant cousins do marry. I believe it happens with some frequency. There are several examples in Collinsport."

Greta was looking out at the ocean again with dreamy eyes. "I have been so weary lately. But I'm not anymore. I can only think of what a wonderful summer it is going to be."

The idyllic moment was interrupted as Luke Sinnot came hurrying around the end of the house, heading directly toward them. As he reached the summer house Margaret saw that his face was twisted with anger. This was not usual.

She stood up to question him. "Whatever is wrong, Luke?"

"Him!" Luke said angrily and touched a hand to his jaw. "That man who has come to the old house. He knocked me down."

"You mean Hare? Cousin Barnabas' servant?" Margaret asked.

Luke nodded. "Hare came at me and he knocked me down." Greta now joined in the conversation. "But he must have had some reason, Luke. Why?"

The hulking young handyman looked shamefaced and didn't reply for a moment. Then he said, "I went for some clay pots I had stacked in the shed."

"But you were told to keep away from the old house," Greta reminded him.

Luke looked stubbornly sullen. "The clay pots was there. I had need of them."

Margaret felt she should try to explain. "But these people have rented the house, shed and all. And they asked not to be disturbed. Hare can't hear or speak. He wouldn't know why you were looking in the shed."

"He had no cause to knock me down," Luke persisted.

"That is true," Margaret agreed. "And I'll mention this to Cousin Barnabas and see if he won't let you go and get the clay pots. In the meantime, please do stay away from the old house."

"Yes ma'am," Luke said, not too happily.

"And now isn't it time for Luke to take you for your regular morning visit about the place?" she asked Greta.

Her daughter looked strangely uninterested. "I don't really want to go."

"I think you should," Margaret said. "It will do you good and take Luke's mind off his troubles." She turned to the retarded man. "You do want to wheel Miss Greta around for a bit, don't you?"

Luke's problems were lost in smiling anticipation as he came up to grasp the wheelchair in his powerful hands. "Yes, ma'am," he said happily.

Margaret returned to her chair and watched them as they went across the lawn. Things were changing swiftly at Collinwood. The placid routine of the old estate had been broken by the arrival of Cousin Barnabas, and it was not liable to be ever the same again. As she resumed her needlework a chill of apprehension crept through her. Could she manage this new situation and give her daughter protection?

In the afternoon Clare Blandish came for tea, which provided a pleasant change for both Margaret and her daughter. Although younger by ten years than Margaret, the attractive raven-haired Clare was a widow. She had married a rather elderly Collinsport man who had left her childless and wealthy. But Clare was a remarkable young woman and had quickly filled the void in her life by turning her large home into a private orphanage. For several years now she had offered refuge to a dozen children between the age of a few months and their early teens. As soon as she managed to place one for adoption she took in another.

And as they all sat over their teacups in the Collins living room that afternoon Clare was full of news about the latest addition to the orphanage.

"A sweet child of nine," she told them. "She came to me from up Bangor way. Such a darling!" She turned to smile at Greta. "And so pretty! Although she's just a baby I think in many ways she resembles you."

Greta was charmed by this idea. "I'd like to meet her."

"You shall," Clare promised. "I'll arrange to bring her over some day."

Margaret thought quickly. Greta had shown a definite interest in this child who was supposed to look like her. Why not use this as an antidote for her girlish crush on Cousin Barnabas? If her attention could be diverted to the child, she would have less time to mope romantically about her distant cousin. She said, "Why not have the child stay with us for a few days? I'm sure it would be a welcome diversion for all of us."

Clare Blandish showed some surprise. "Perhaps she might enjoy it. But would Jonas approve? I know how severe he is. He has little patience with children."

"But you say the girl is nine," Margaret pointed out. "I trust she has good manners. She should present no problem."

"I don't believe she would," Clare agreed with a pleased smile. "While she has spirit, she is quiet and polite for the most part."

Greta smiled. "I think it would be wonderful. How exciting to have another new face here! And I'm sure Cousin Barnabas would enjoy seeing a child here."

Clare raised her eyebrows in delicate surprise. "Cousin Barnabas? Who is he?"

Margaret put down her tea cup. "I don't believe we mentioned him. He has just arrived from England." And she proceeded to explain.

Greta capped her explanation with, "He's a most fascinating man!"

Clare Blandish showed interest. "I'm sure he sounds so. I look forward to meeting him."

"You must," Margaret agreed, thinking this would be at least a beginning in introducing Barnabas to the village. "Unfortunately he is rarely around during the daylight hours. He is a scientist and engaged on some important work while he is here."

"What sort of work?" Clare wanted to know.

"It's a secret," Greta said. "But we all think it must be terribly difficult and of great moment."

"He is likely to visit us in the evening," Margaret told her guest. "Please do stop by after dinner sometime. As I say, he probably won't join us while there is any light left in the sky. He seems to take his work very seriously."

"I'll remember," Clare promised as she rose to leave. "And I'll also see about bringing Judith over. That is the name of the child I mentioned."

Margaret hoped the arrival of the child at Collinwood might be a healthy counterbalance to the coming of Barnabas. But she warned Greta not to mention the child's coming to her father. Jonas would condemn the plan without giving it consideration and she did not want that.

Once again Barnabas Collins presented himself at the house shortly after dusk. Margaret thought he appeared just a trifle nervous but he was as kind and attentive to Greta as he had been before. The melancholy cast of his gaunt, handsome face was pronounced as he sat close to the invalid girl and spoke of his years in London.

Margaret sat quietly and listened. Barnabas seemed to have had a wide collection of friends and to have lived the life of a wealthy English gentleman. But there was something about him that left her with a feeling of unrest. She couldn't be certain what it was; perhaps it was many things.

Certainly it was odd that he should sit there with the rather heavy caped coat on. And when she had greeted him at the door she'd noticed that the touch of his hand was still icy. Now as she watched him fondle the silver wolf's-head cane as he talked she saw that the palms of each of his hands had tufts of coarse black hairs. There was something repulsive in this revelation.

Even though she knew it was unfair to hold such a minor physical blemish against him, she found it bothered her. And it made her study the hands clasped on the cane head more closely. They appeared to have a claw-like look and the unusual black ring on the forefinger of his right hand only served to highlight their ugliness. The hands were in contrast to his rather attractive if hollow-cheeked countenance and she wondered if they were the key to his true self. They looked so much older than his face and had a ghastly corpselike appearance.

The thought shocked her so she lost the thread of his account of a fine London shop. It was too weirdly true! She had seen just such hands clasped across the bosom of a corpse as it rested in a coffin. She tried to banish the thought from her mind and concentrate on what he was saying. But now she knew what bothered her. This dark, charming man seated opposite her had the whiff of the grave about him, the suggestion that he was not in good health and might soon die. And yet he had seemed powerful enough when he'd managed Greta's wheelchair.

Barnabas Collins fixed his hypnotic eyes on her and said, "Your husband is at his office again. He rarely spends an evening at home, it seems."

Margaret smiled apologetically. "He is too ambitious, Cousin Barnabas. His desire for wealth has devoured him."

"It is a common ailment," Barnabas said with a grave smile. "It is too bad. You and your lovely daughter must find it lonesome."

Greta smiled from her chair. "That is why your coming has meant so much to us, Barnabas."

He turned to her with a kindly expression. "I, too, am gaining by my visit here. I have become very weary of the great outside world."

Margaret said, "Your experiments, Cousin Barnabas, are they of a very special nature? I suppose I should not be so curious. But both Greta and I have wondered."

"That is quite understandable," he said, giving her his full attention once again. The deep-set eyes bored into her as he continued with great gravity. "I am embarked on the ultimate quest of man. The secret of rejuvenation. The elixir of eternal youth."

Margaret gasped. "What an audacious undertaking!"

He smiled grimly. "Audacious and ambitious. But I am well on my way. That is why I must guard my work so closely. What I already have discovered would be considered worth a king's ransom."

Greta studied him anxiously. "Then you do expect to be engaged in your experiments a long time? You won't be leaving us soon."

"I shall be remaining here a considerable time," Barnabas assured her.

"I'm so glad to hear that," Greta said with relief.

"Yes," Margaret interposed, to prevent her daughter from revealing too clearly her great affection for the newcomer from England. "We look forward to having you meet some of our friends. Clare Blandish, for instance." And she went on to tell him about the wealthy young widow.

Barnabas listened with obvious interest. "She sounds charming," he said. "And I should enjoy seeing this ward of hers, as well. The child Judith, who so resembles you, Greta."

Greta laughed self-consciously. "Just as I'm supposed to look like the long-dead Josette."

The gaunt man nodded slowly as he considered this. "Exactly." He got up from his chair and went over to gaze at the portrait above the sideboard again.

"That portrait fascinates you, Cousin Barnabas," Greta said.

His broad caped back was to them and he did not reply for a moment. Then very slowly he turned with a far-away expression on his hollow-cheeked face. "You are right," he said. "She possesses a very special type of beauty. Just as you do." And he walked back to the chair to study Greta as intently as he had the painting.

Margaret felt her nerves on edge. She rose from her chair, saying, "It is past your bedtime, Greta."

"Not yet!" her daugher protested.

Barnabas turned to Margaret with one of his engaging smiles. "At least not until I have taken her for a turn around the garden. It is such a lovely night. And warmer than before."

Margaret did not like this at all. She moved forward a step to protest. "Really, I don't think!"

"Mother, don't try to spoil everything!" Greta said, with a distressed look on her pretty face. "Please take me out now, Cousin Barnabas."

Without waiting for further permission he wheeled the chair toward the foyer. Margaret followed a few steps behind, desperately searching for some reasonable excuse to prevent this becoming an established pattern.

They passed the great mirror by the door and as she casually glanced into it she was suddenly shocked to the point that she halted and let the others go on ahead. She couldn't believe what she had seen! Of course it was an optical illusion made easily acceptable by her ragged state of nerves. But when she'd looked into the mirror there had been no reflection of Barnabas Collins at all!

It had seemed that the wheelchair with Greta in it was being propelled forward on its own. The figure of Barnabas had simply not shown in the mirror. But it was too ridiculous. She touched a hand to her temple, feeling faint. She was allowing herself to harbor ridiculous thoughts.

Now she went out to the foyer and saw that they had already left. Too late to do anything about it now. Wringing her hands nervously, she made her way to the nearest window and peered out. But she could see no sign of them. And then to further torment her jagged nerves a dog began to howl mournfully in the distance. This touch of eerie melancholy was the last thing she needed. She felt ready to scream.

She paced up and down in the foyer as she waited. And once she paused in front of the portrait of the first Barnabas Collins and felt the painting had taken on a faintly sardonic, mocking expression. How alike this other Barnabas was to the one who had left Collinwood so long ago! She must follow Greta's advice and see if she could find some information about him and the others of his day in the papers locked in the desk in her husband's library.

Then she heard the sound of the wheelchair being eased up the stairs and opened the door to let Greta and Cousin Barnabas in. Her daughter was in the same ecstatic mood as on the previous evening. It was evident no harm had come to her. Barnabas again kissed her daughter's hand and said goodnight. And it distressed Margaret that this almost stranger had so won her daughter's affection.

As she helped prepare Greta for bed, she warned her, "You seem very weak again tonight. This business of staying up late and entertaining Cousin Barnabas has to end."

"No, Mother!" Greta's pretty face became firm.

"But I'm only thinking about your health," Margaret protested, gazing down at her invalid daughter in bed.

Greta stared up at her from her pillow. "I think you're jealous, Mother, because he gives me more attention than he does you."

"What nonsense!" she said. But at the same time she knew she was blushing. How would she have behaved if Cousin Barnabas had showed her the same ardent attention? It had been so long since Jonas had given her any sign of affection that she was starved for love. Would she not have become enamored of the handsome English cousin as easily as her daughter if Barnabas had wooed her in the same way? The realization shocked her so she bade her daughter a hasty goodnight and left the room as quickly as she could.

The next morning it was foggy, with a drizzle of rain. Margaret was glad of this, for she was able to persuade Greta to remain in bed and take a much-needed rest. It also left her free for an undertaking she had promised herself—to go through the old documents locked in the rolltop desk in a corner of the library. She had an extra key for it and since Jonas put little stock in such things, she was sure he would not care if she went through the collection of papers.

When she unlocked the desk she found there were more items poked in its many compartments then she'd imagined. To make her task more difficult, there seemed to be no order to them. They'd simply been stuffed away and forgotten. Quite a few of the notebooks, diaries and letters were of fairly recent vintage. But as she sifted through some of the later items she did come upon a diary written by a Pastor Arnold Collins in the eighteen hundred and forties. From this account she learned that at least one of the Collins family had taken Holy Orders. This Pastor Arnold Collins lived in Boston where he had his church, but came to Collinsport for his vacations. And while in the old house had started to assemble notes for a history of the family.

Margaret frowned as she turned several pages of the dead clergyman's writing that dealt long-windedly with church problems of the day and had no bearing on the family. Then she came to an entry that caught her attention.

"July 8th, 1846. On this day did make certain discoveries bound to be of great value in compiling our family history. Several letters from Joshua Collins to a friend concerning the sad case of his son, Barnabas, have come my way. Dark undertones to these letters. I suspect witchcraft!"

She found her heart beating faster as she read these words. What could they mean? Had this scholar found some terrible secret about his forebears? She read on but there was no further reference to the letters or the family history. It was several pages later that the old clergyman again returned to this subject.

"July 24th, 1846. The family history. I have talked with others and read Joshua Collins' letters carefully. And I am convinced that his son Barnabas left Collinsport under a cloud. This handsome son met some tragic fate which, while not plainly stated, seems linked with the powers of darkness. There is horror and fear in his father's letters and the suggestion that Barnabas forfeited his soul to the Devil."

The entry closed abruptly on this note. And again Margaret had to wade through a series of dull entries having nothing to do with Barnabas Collins or the family history. And then at the bottom of a page she was frustrated to read a terse message in a different handwriting.

"August 3rd, 1846. Pastor Arnold Collins found dead on this day."

She had come to a blind alley. With the death of the old clergyman there were no additional entries. Whatever he had learned appeared to have died with him. And how had he come to his death? Had it been of natural causes or a violent end? The terse entry in the diary was not of much help. It simply stated he had been found dead. But Margaret couldn't stop conjuring up visions of the old man having been attacked by some dread thing.

Had he discovered too much? So much that the evil had closed in on him and demanded his life? She began searching the other papers and journals, but found no references to Barnabas or his father, Joshua. At last she locked the desk up once more and left the library, suffering from a violent headache.

She went directly to her own room and stretched out on the bed. The slow drizzle outside had turned into a steady rain. As it beat down in a heavy tattoo against the roof and the trees by her window she tried to put all the wild thoughts out of her mind and get a little rest. But she couldn't. The ancient diary had filled her with fear and misgivings without filling her in on the facts in any way. It was too frustrating.

Then there came a soft knock at her door, so gentle that at first she did not hear it. When it came a second time she got up from the bed and went over and opened the door to reveal a frightened-looking Ada standing there.

"Yes, Ada," she said, staring at the maid.

"May I speak to you a minute, ma'am?" the girl asked abjectly.

"Yes, of course," Margaret said, standing back for her to enter.

The girl came in. "I'm sorry to trouble you, ma'am."

Margaret closed the door to give them privacy. "Well, what is it, Ada?"

Ada swallowed hard, her hands working nervously at the lace frill of her apron. "It's about Patience, ma'am."

"Yes," Margaret said, wondering what the girl could have to tell her about the other maid. Usually the sisters were inseparable and always stood up for each other.

Ada looked desperately unhappy. "I don't mean to cause any trouble for her, ma'am. But I'm near out of my mind with worry about her."

"Please explain yourself, Ada," Margaret said in a kindly way.

"It's about that man!"

"What man?"

"Him that has come from England. That Barnabas!" Ada's young face showed fear. "You remember how he met her the first night he came. She fell and he helped her get up."

"Yes."

Ada gave her a wide-eyed look. "Well, she has been meeting him every night since."

Margaret was astonished. "Are you certain?"

"Yes, ma'am. We share the same room. And she gets up in the middle of the night and leaves it. Like she was sleepwalking. I watched from the window and she always meets him."

"This happens regularly?"

"Yes."

"Are you sure she is met by Barnabas Collins?"

The girl nodded. "Yes, I couldn't miss that cape. They walk off toward the old house. Sometimes she is gone two hours or more. I've pretended to be asleep when she comes back. I've been afraid to speak to her. She seems to be in a sort of dream. And when the morning comes and I ask her what she's been doing she denies ever being out of the house."

Margaret was increasingly upset. "She claims she didn't meet Barnabas?"

"Yes. She says I've been dreaming it all. But I know I haven't."

"Dreams can be extremely vivid," Margaret warned her. "Are you sure you haven't been having recurrent nightmares?"

"Yes, ma'am," the girl said, frightened but determined. "I know that because of her throat."

"Her throat?"

Ada swallowed hard again. "The red marks on it. Like giant bites spaced a little apart. They are always there in the morning and fade away during the day. She keeps a cloth around her throat to hide them. But they are there every morning!"

Margaret could not question the certainty in Ada's tone. And what was more frightening she remembered noticing the bandage around the neck of the attractive Patience.

She caught her breath!

For she also recalled those weird marks she'd seen on her own daughter's neck. And now she realized there was some sinister link between the two.

CHAPTER 4

Staring straight ahead at the rain creasing down the window pane she asked in a tense voice, "What do you make of those marks, Ada?"

"I don't rightly know, ma'am," the girl said. "But Granny Entwhistle calls them the Devil's kiss."

"'The Devil's kiss?'"

"Yes, ma'am," Ada went on excitedly. "She says that long ago she was told there were a rash of such happenings here in Collinsport. And it ended with some of the girls from the village being throttled before the Devil vanished."

Margaret gave the girl's anxious face a quick look. "But you must know that Granny is very old—she imagines all sorts of impossible things."

"Yes, ma'am," Ada said uneasily.

Margaret knew she had to appear casual. "I'm sure," she said briskly, "there will be a quite normal explanation for the marks you've seen on Patience's throat. Perhaps a fever or some insect bites may be the answer."

"Yes, ma'am," Ada replied, without seeming at all convinced.

"I promise I'll give this some thought and perhaps later speak to Patience about it."

"I wish you would, ma'am," Ada worried. "Patience is a good girl. And she has never lied to me about anything. I don't think she knows what is happening. Her going out in the night and such. I'm afraid for her."

Margaret forced a smile. "That is commendable of you, Ada. Just leave it to me."

Once she was alone her own doubts and fears grew alarmingly. It was all right to tell the girl that everything that had gone on could be explained normally. But she no longer believed this herself.

What was the secret of Barnabas Collins? For these unexplainable incidents had surely begun with his arrival. And why had she been apprehensive about the handsome, gaunt man ever since his coming? He had been charming enough. And his kindness to Greta had been disarming. And he had won her daughter's heart to the point that she was obviously dreaming of marriage.

This had taken place in an incredibly short time. Barnabas had come to Collinwood and changed everything instantly. Was this business of the nightly meetings with Patience nothing but a vulgar affair between the two? Or did it signify something more diabolical?

Margaret had moved to the window and was now standing staring out at the old house in the distance. It had an evil, brooding look on this rainy dark afternoon. She was allowing her imagination to run riot on the basis of a few remarks by an ignorant village girl. And yet there were things she had herself encountered in these past days which defied rational explanation!

The huge bat which had blundered through the window on the night of the arrival of Barnabas to threaten and harass her. Jonas had doubted its existence, perhaps understandably. Bats of such a size were alien to this Maine coast. But she had seen it, smelled the fetid odor of its smothering outspread wings, had crouched in fear and tried to protect herself from it. It was surely real to her!

But it had vanished at the sound of Jonas approaching. Vanished much too quickly. And then there had been that other incredible moment when she'd looked into the mirror and Barnabas had not been reflected there. He should have been, no matter how she tried to explain it. And those eyes of his! There were times when he looked at her and she was unable to marshal her thoughts properly. Surely he must possess some weird hypnotic power.

Of course her main concern was her daughter. Greta had to be protected, no matter what. And Barnabas had already gone far to win the lonely girl's affection. It was too late now to take any harsh direct action; this would only turn her daughter against her. She must conduct this struggle to take care of Greta's safety in a subtle manner.

The mention of those weird marks were what had really frightened her most. They had surely appeared on Greta's throat after she'd been out alone with Cousin Barnabas on that first night. Margaret couldn't be sure whether they had shown again or not. It seemed like incredible carelessness in retrospect, but she'd been too generally upset to notice.

The Devil's kiss, Granny Entwhistle had called them. Well, Granny might know more about what was going on than anyone else. Margaret left her room and went down the corridor to mount the steps to the tiny attic room occupied by the old woman.

The door to the room was shut, but Margaret knocked on it and waited a moment for an answer. When none came she tried the doorknob and opened the door. In the shadowed room she saw the old woman seated in a rocking chair by the single small window, her ancient head slumped forward on her chest and her eyes closed in sleep.

Margaret moved quietly to her side. Touching the old woman's shoulder, she said gently, "Granny!"

Her head stirred and her wrinkled face turned to Margaret. The rheumy sunken eyes gradually focused and the toothless mouth became firmer.

"Yes, ma'am?" She made an effort as if to get up.

Margaret pressed her back in the chair. "Please don't move, Granny," she said. "I just wanted to speak to you a moment. To ask you a question or two."

"Parson Collins will be coming on the stage tonight," the old woman murmured tonelessly. "The table must be set for a round dozen and I have scarce time to prepare." Margaret frowned. Parson Collins! It brought back the diary she had been reading earlier. She knew the old woman had been dreaming and was still lost in the demi-world between dream and reality. Granny Entwhistle was old enough to have been in service at the old mansion when Parson Collins came for his annual summer holiday.

She said, "Did you know Parson Collins?"

Granny gave her a vague glance. "I knew him until the Devil struck him dead. Found in his bed staring up at the ceiling with open eyes full of fear. I was there when they found him. A shock, the doctor said it was. But we all knew better. It were the Devil's business!"

"Why do you say that?"

Granny's wizened face took on a cunning look. "Because Parson Collins had found out more than he should! So the old Devil silenced him!"

Margaret fought hard to keep her calm and question the old woman carefully. "What had he found out?"

"About Barnabas, Angelique and the curse!"

It was all fitting in with what she'd read in the diary. Margaret knelt by the old woman's chair and with a concerned look on her attractive matronly face she begged, "Do tell me what the curse was."

Again that crafty look spread across Granny's face. She smiled in a far-away manner. "Not for the likes of me to say."

"You must try to remember," Margaret insisted. "It's important that I know. Important for Greta's safety." She knew the old woman loved Greta.

This seemed to rouse her. She nodded gravely. "Poor little dear! So the curse reached out to her! And she the spitting image of Josette, rest her soul!"

"Tell me about this curse. Has it anything to do with the Devil's kiss?"

The rheumy eyes fixed on her warily. "It is the Devil's kiss!"

Margaret tried to make it all fit. The curse was the Devil's kiss! What could this have to do with the marks on the throats of Patience and her daughter? What did "the Devil's kiss" signify?

She said, "Please tell me more. I don't understand you."

Granny's wrinkled face became sullen. "They are all sluggards. No one listens to me. A round dozen coming and nothing ready!" She was back in that kitchen of long ago lamenting lack of preparations for the expected guests —guests who were now years dead and buried.

"What was the curse placed upon Barnabas?" Margaret persisted.

"The witch did it!" Granny said, her reply coming with surprising clarity. "Angelique was the witch! He and sweet Josette were the ones who suffered! And all that came after them!"

Granny's head slumped forward again and there was the sound of gentle snoring. Despite Margaret's anxiety, she knew it would be useless to question her further for the moment. Very quietly she rose and left the room. She had not found out much. Something horrible had happened in the old house years ago, and it had ended with Josette a suicide and Barnabas becoming a wanderer. And yet Granny had insisted the curse remained a dark threat to Collinwood and all those who bore the Collins name. Had it begun to work now that a descendant of that first Barnabas had returned? And was this new Barnabas Collins as much a victim of the curse as any of them?

The rain gave way to a heavy fog as the dinner hour approached. Greta, looking rested and much better, insisted on leaving her room. Margaret scrutinized her daughter's throat closely as she helped her dress, but could make out no hint of the sinister red marks. She suspected that some of her daughter's zeal to appear at the dinner table was linked with a desire to be ready and waiting if Barnabas should make his usual appearance in the early evening. Margaret hoped he would not come and was thankful that at least the weather was in her favor. He could not suggest taking Greta out around the grounds on this miserable night.

As they sat at the table in the wood-paneled dining room, an ornate hanging lamp casting its warm glow over the gleaming white cloth, the silver and china, she thought she had never seen Greta look more lovely. And her eyes moved to the portrait above the sideboard for a comparison with the unhappy Josette. There was no doubt that Greta did resemble the long dead girl.

Greta paused over her dinner to tell her father, "Cousin Barnabas wants to take me to England one day. He had an apartment in the heart of London."

Jonas regarded her grouchily from the head of the table. "I should think he'd know better than to fill your head with such fancies."

"But I will go!" Greta said, at once looking forlorn. "Cousin Barnabas doesn't think I should limit myself because I happen to be a cripple!"

"Then he is an idiot!" her father said caustically. "And I would prefer not to hear him quoted incessantly. He has only been here a few days and one would assume a new book had been added to the Holy Scriptures, Cousin Barnabas!"

"Come now!" Margaret reproved her husband. "You mustn't be so irritable. Barnabas has only been trying to cheer Greta up. And I see no reason why she shouldn't travel. It would do us all good to have a change. Why don't the three of us take passage on one of the Collins ships to England?"

"Because we no longer operate a sailing service across the Atlantic, for one thing." Jonas glared at her. "You don't seem to be aware that we are quickly becoming a fishing company. That salt cod pack is what I'm counting on to recoup the family fortunes. And doing fairly well at, despite a complete lack of interest on your part."

"You know I always take great pleasure in your achievements," Margaret said placatingly. "It is only that I regret your diligence gives you scant time for Greta and me."

Greta nodded. "This is such a lonesome house. That is why Cousin Barnabas' coming here has meant so much to me." Her face brightened. "And I look forward to the little girl Clare is bringing to to stay with us."

"Not now, Greta," Margaret said with a warning look, knowing it was too late.

Jonas was sitting back in his chair scowling at her. "Did I hear right? Am I to understand you are taking in one of Clare's stray brats?"

"Just for a short time, Jonas," his wife said quickly. "It's because the child bears a strong likeness to our Greta."

"Indeed," Jonas said sarcastically. "I can imagine that is typical of Clare's exaggerations to trap us into providing a home for one of her ill-assorted brood!"

"You're so unfair, Father," Greta told him. "I think Clare is doing a wonderful work. And we all should help her."

Jonas Collins rose from the table. "Charity, my dear, begins at home. You will discover that for yourself one day." And turning to Margaret, he added, "I trust this unfortunate arrangement has not gone too far to be canceled."

"I'll speak to Clare," Margaret promised him.

"I shall count on you to do that," Jonas said grimly, and marched out of the dining room.

Greta looked at her mother with dismay as soon as they were alone. "I hope I didn't spoil it!"

"You knew your father would be displeased. I warned you!"

"I forgot for a moment," Greta said unhappily. "But you still will let the child come no matter what Father says?"

"I shall do my best," Margaret said wearily.

"The weather is so awful tonight," Greta said disconsolately. "Do you think Cousin Barnabas will visit us?"

"I'm sure I can't say," her mother told her.

"I hope he does. I count on him so. He's so different from Father."

"You mustn't mind your father," Margaret told her as she got up from the table to wheel her daughter out of the dining room. "Although he may seem gruff and cold I can promise you he loves you a great deal."

Greta sighed. "He has a poor way of showing it."

Margaret was in full agreement with this, although she didn't dare to say so. The hard nature of Jonas had done enough harm. No wonder that the lonely invalid responded so fully to the kindness and charm Barnabas showered on her. Well, Barnabas must have a good side to be so considerate.

But what of the other part of his nature? Was he concealing

his second self, a coarse brutal person who was not above nightly dalliance with a kitchen maid? Who encouraged her daughter to think he was in love with her while he was having regular meetings with another?

She left Greta in the living room to watch out the window while she went on out to the kitchen. Granny Entwhistle was seated close to the great wood stove, dozing in its warmth. A large kettle of water boiled on the stove and Ada and Patience were busy washing the dishes at an oversize sink.

Margaret approached them, reserving her closest scrutiny for Patience. It struck her that the girl seemed unduly pale. Otherwise she appeared quite herself, smiling brightly when she saw Margaret.

"You're looking very white," Margaret told her. "I trust you haven't been ill?"

"On the contrary, ma'am," the girl said. "I feel very well."

Margaret was aware the other girl was taking in this exchange with more than casual interest. Ada pretended to be very busy scrubbing a pan as Margaret went on questioning her sister. "Have you been getting lots of rest? No broken sleep."

"Indeed, ma'am, I'm a sound sleeper as Ada will tell you," Patience said with a smile.

Margaret's eyebrows lifted. And she looked directly at Ada. "Is that true? Does Patience sleep well?"

Ada, looking miserable, said carefully, "She has always been one to enjoy a sound sleep, ma'am."

Margaret knew the girl was merely saying this because she believed that Patience was somehow not aware of her midnight trysts with Barnabas, that these interludes smacked of sleepwalking. So she merely commented, "Well, you must not work too hard, Patience. You look somewhat peaked."

"Thank you, ma'am," the girl said politely. "But I'm sure there is nothing to worry yourself about."

Margaret left the kitchen wishing she was as confirmed in this belief as the pretty little maid. She was now inclined to agree with Ada that Patience was meeting Barnabas in a sort of trance. It began to seem suspiciously certain that the newcomer from London was exerting some sinister hypnotic spell over her.

And had he also extended the same terrifying power over her own daughter! Greta was surely a different girl since she had known him. It seemed that her whole existence had come to depend on him. Margaret frowned at the realization knowing how wrong and dangerous it was.

Why, she asked herself, had this modern descendant of the first Barnabas returned to Collinwood? And what were the mysterious experiments that occupied him all the daytime hours? He had spoken of an elixir of youth, a goal so outlandish she doubted if it were true. But something did chain him to the old house during the day. If she knew what it was she might know a great deal more about Barnabas.

Pausing in the shadowed rear hallway before returning to her daughter she suddenly remembered the side cellar door of the old house. She had a key to it. And it struck her if one were very careful it might be possible to use that entrance without attracting any notice.

The idea appealed to her. It was likely that Barnabas Collins would still be at work there now. It was a full half-hour until dusk. And if she made a quiet entry into the old building she might learn what he was filling his days with.

There was a rough, dark cape hanging from a nail in the hallway that was used by any of the kitchen help when they had to make a journey across the yard in inclement weather. She reached up and took it, thinking it would be ideal for her use now. And then she went to the sideboard where she kept her keys and found the one she needed.

Making sure she'd not been noticed by anyone, she hurriedly stepped out into the fog. It was starting to get dark early because of the heavy mist that shrouded everything. It was also coolish and she shivered as she hurried out of sight of the kitchen windows and past the outbuildings. When she drew near the old house she moved close to the bushes and made her way around to it from the rear.

The house was as silent and seemingly empty of life as usual. Carefully she knelt by the wooden doors protecting the cellar entrance and fitted the iron key into the rusty padlock. For a moment it seemed that it would not turn. Then, with a creaking protest, the rust-coated lock opened. She removed it from the iron flanges on the door and very carefully lifted one of the wooden sides to reveal a steep set of stone steps that led directly to the dark cellar.

Too late she realized she had forgotten to provide herself with matches or a candle. She would have to brave that darkness unaided if she went on down there. But there was no question of hesitating or turning back now. Quickly she dodged down the steps and then drew the wooden door back closed. It left her in total darkness. She lingered on the remaining steps a moment, waiting for her eyes to become a bit better adjusted to the black around her.

The old house was familiar to her and she now concentrated on recalling the layout of the cellar and the several stairways that led to the upper regions of the first home of the Collins family. Reaching out to touch the damp wall, she gingerly went down the last steps until her feet were on the earthen floor of the cellar.

Down here it smelled of mildew, dust and rotting wood. The cellar had not been used for some time. The elderly schoolteacher who had last rented the house had made no use of it at all. By keeping one hand against the stone wall of the foundation she made her way along the length of the shadowed tomblike area without too much difficulty. All at once she stumbled against the bottom of a stairway. She caught herself and stood very still, momentarily holding her breath, as she listened to discover if she'd been heard.

It seemed she hadn't, for there was no response to the noise she'd made. Hare, of course, was deaf and dumb so she need have no fear of him unless he happened to see her. It was Barnabas Collins she needed to be wary of. She could imagine his anger if he found her intruding. But she had no choice; Greta must be protected. And to do that she must find out additional facts about this stranger from England who had so taken over at Collinwood.

Slowly, a step at a time, she mounted the rickety wooden stairway that led to a hallway running the length of the house. As she recalled it, the stairs ended at a door about midway down the hall. It would give her an excellent spot from which to inspect the first floor of the house and from which to move on to any further investigations it might seem desirable to make. At last she was on the top step. Again she listened but could hear no sound of movement on the other side of the door.

Drawing on all her courage, she slowly turned the knob and opened the door. The dark hallway, like all the rest of the house, was cloaked in a deathly silence. The corridor floor was of broad boards and uncarpeted. She went on with great caution, knowing that at any moment Hare or Barnabas might come swooping down on her. Keeping close to the wall, she made her way to the front living room of the old mansion.

One of the double doors was ajar slightly and she was able to peer in at the gloomy splendor. The great cut-glass chandelier and the fine old furniture set the tone of the room. And she saw that a table had been set with a white cloth in the middle of the room with places for two. Two candles in silver sticks graced the table and it was evident Barnabas had either been entertaining or expected to entertain a guest there. She could not believe it had been set this way for himself and Hare.

And then she frowned as she noticed something draped over the back of one of the chairs. She could not make out what it was, merely that it was of shining white material. Her curiosity overcoming her caution, she edged forward a step at a time until she reached the chair and lifted the garment so casually set out there. Her amazement grew as examination proved to be a rich gown in the style of another century. It even had the odor of age about it. And as she held it up before her she was struck with the thought that it could easily have been a wedding gown!

Quickly returning it to the back of the chair, she moved out into the hallway again. The room across from the living room seemed not to be in use. The shutters kept out all outside light and the furniture was draped with ghostly covers. She stood there a moment deciding what to do next when there came the sound of a heavy measured footstep on the upper stairs. This left her no choice. She ran for the door by which she'd entered. And then she hastily made her way back down the rickety steps to the dank bowels of the cellar.

Terrified, Margaret pressed herself against the cellar wall and waited, praying that whoever it was would not come down there. The heavy tread had sounded suspiciously like that of the brutal, hulking Hare. She pictured the cruel face with its flat receding forehead and tried to imagine his reaction if he found her there. It would be violent. She was sure of that.

Now the footsteps sounded directly above her. And from the other end of the cellar a door opened a moment or so later and a light showed. She moved so that she was under the steps and partly screened by them and watched and waited.

There was the sound of a throat being roughly cleared and then the squat, heavy figure of Hare showed on the other stairway. He was holding a lantern whose shade was badly smoked and he came down slowly. Yet there was purpose in his movements. She had an idea he knew exactly where he was going. This was no casual examination of the cellar area he was engaging in.

She watched with horrified fascination as he came down the length of the cellar in her direction. She held her breath as she drew back expecting at any moment the sullen figure would hold up the lantern and she would be revealed. But when he was close to her he veered his direction and went to a spot about ten feet away. He stood there fumbling for a moment, his free hand groping against the wall. And then all at once he apparently touched a release and a panel opened in front of him, revealing an inner room.

By leaning forward she was able to get a glimpse of the room into which he stepped. The secret room behind the hidden panel. And in the indifferent light of the lantern she saw that it was barren of furnishings except for a coffin set up in its far corner!

A coffin with a closed lid and two lighted candles at its head! She had to fight to restrain the cry of terror that automatically formed on her lips. It was at that moment Hare came back and closed the panel, remaining inside. She could see no more.

The brief glimpse of the secret room had baffled her. She had never known there was one in the old house. Of course there had been vague rumors of secret stairways but Jonas had stoutly denied such ever existed. No need for further denials; she had just seen one such hidden chamber with her own eyes. But could she believe what had been revealed there?

It seemed too incredible! The Collins family would not have a hidden tomb there. The family burial ground was a distance beyond the old house on the edge of a woods. Yet she had watched Hare lumbering toward the closed coffin and he had not appeared at all surprised by it. He was in there with it now.

Did this have any bearing on Barnabas' experiments? He had said his work dealt with the secret of youth. The secret of life, perhaps? She could only wonder. But this unexpected revelation had added to the badly frayed state of her nerves. She drew the cloak about her, hoping it would help to hide her in the murky cellar.

How soon would Hare emerge from the secret room? Dare she try to leave now? Or should she stop to see if anything more of the mystery of the old house might be revealed to her. As she waited in the darkness she grew more and more uneasy. It seemed foolhardy to stay there on the small chance she might get additional information. The real danger was that Hare would emerge from the room and discover her. She left her place under the stairway and started back to the other stone steps that led above ground. The passage along the cellar seemed to take an endless time. And as she reached the stone steps she was certain she heard a rustle in the darkness behind her.

This brought her close to hysterics. She scrambled up the uneven moss-covered steps to heave the wooden door back and rush out into the foggy night. As she hurled the wooden door back in place she realized the noise it made would betray her. Filled with sudden panic, she raced through the darkness toward the main house. And then she heard the footsteps coming close behind her! Overtaking her!

CHAPTER 5

Margaret ran on. Sheer terror had seized her now. And as she veered occasionally from the path she found the grass wet and slippery under her feet. Her pursuer was still close behind and she had a good distance to go before even reaching the outbuildings. Then, without warning, she slipped and fell with hands outstretched. She had lost her chance to escape.

Before she could struggle to her feet again her pursuer was standing over her. She dared not look up, fearful of what she might see.

"What made you run so, ma'am?" It was the retarded Luke's voice.

In complete amazement she stared up at the unkempt figure of the handyman. "You frightened me when you came running after me!"

Luke's expressionless face gave no hint that he understood the situation. He said, "You came out of the old house. Out from the cellar. I followed you."

Margaret was standing facing him in the mist-shrouded darkness. She told him earnestly, "Please don't mention this to anyone, Luke. Do you understand? You didn't see me at all tonight."

"I didn't see you," Luke repeated stupidly.

"You didn't see me near the old house or anywhere else.

Remember that, no matter who asks you."

Luke nodded, seeming to get her message. "Yes, ma'am."

"It's very important, Luke. Miss Greta's safety may depend on it."

"Yes, ma'am. I was afraid that Hare would get you."

"Don't worry about Hare," she said. "And keep away from the old house. I don't want you to have any trouble with that wretched man."

"I watch the house from the bushes," Luke volunteered. "Hare goes in and out but I never see the other one. The one with the black cape."

Margaret listened to him, thinking about what she'd just undergone in the dank cellar of the old house. The secret room and its coffin with the lighted candles at its head still haunted her. What did it mean? And where had Barnabas been all the time she was there? She had seen only the ugly Hare.

She told Luke, "Don't worry about it. I'm going back to the main house now. You can come with me part way if you wish."

"Yes, ma'am." Luke seemed to like the idea.

As she moved on towards the lights of the main house he followed a step behind her, remaining close until they arrived at the rear door. Then she paused and turned to him again. "Remember! You haven't seen me."

He looked blank. "Yes, ma'am."

She went inside, still not sure that he had properly understood her. She hoped fervently that he had. She was able to replace the cape without being seen by those in the kitchen. Making an effort at composure, she went back down the hall to rejoin Greta in the living room.

Her daughter was alone in the room in which the only light came from a large lamp on a center table. Greta turned with a wistful expression on her pretty face as Margaret entered through the double doors.

"You have been gone a long time!" Greta accused her. "Where have you been?"

"I had to speak to Ada about some chores and then I talked with Granny Entwhistle," she hastily improvised.

"I've been waiting here alone," Greta said. "Cousin Barnabas hasn't come yet. Do you suppose he's not coming?"

Margaret shrugged. "You make it sound as if it would be a tragedy if he didn't. Must I remind you he is only our tenant and not our guest? Your father has rented the old house to him. We cannot expect him to be at our beck and call. He is busy with his work."

Greta looked hurt. "But I'm certain Cousin Barnabas enjoys

coming here."

"I think we shouldn't assume we know all he is thinking," Margaret warned her.

She was trying hard to create a mood of caution in the girl, and she earnestly hoped that he would not present himself at their door on this miserable, foggy night. She rued the day her husband had decided to accept Barnabas Collins as a tenant.

The minutes ticked by and Margaret began to feel a sense of elation that overcame her previous fear and dismay. But her easy mood was rudely shattered soon after nine when there was a determined knocking on the front door. She glanced at her daughter and saw that Greta's face was radiant.

It was, of course, Barnabas. His shiny raven hair dripped from the wet, as did his black coat. He nodded politely to her with a smile on his gaunt face. If he knew that she'd been in the old house spying on him he gave no indication of it.

"I'm sorry to be late," he said, "especially as I promised your daughter I would try to get here earlier. But my work detained me."

Before Margaret could reply, Greta called out to him from the living room. "I'm in here, Barnabas. Do come and join me."

Barnabas kissed her hand. His eyes fixed intently on her he assured her she looked more beautiful than ever. "It is a miserable night," he continued. "I thought you might enjoy having me read to you. I have noticed some fine books in the library. Perhaps we could go in there so as not to disturb your mother and the others while I read aloud some favorite passages."

Margaret saw the idea as a ruse to get Greta off where he could be alone with her, an alternate to their nightly tour of the grounds. For some reason he wanted to be able to exert his hypnotic influence on her daughter and keep her enthralled with him.

Turning to Greta, she said, "Tonight I think you should retire early. You have not been getting your rest."

"I have been resting all day," Greta protested indignantly. "I want Cousin Barnabas to read to me."

Barnabas spread his hands in a gentle gesture of resignation, which was spoiled for Margaret by the flashing glimpse it offered of the hairy tufts that covered each of his palms. Again she felt a strong revulsion toward the man in black.

He moved forward and grasped Greta's wheelchair. "Please don't worry," he begged Margaret. "I won't keep her long." And he guided the chair down the hallway to the library.

She watched after them feeling a frustration that bordered on despair. After all she'd undergone, she'd discovered very little and Cousin Barnabas had arrived to triumph as always. There was no question but that she must discuss what was going on with Jonas and enlist his help. Surely he would put his daughter's welfare before the pittance of rent he was receiving for the old house? With Jonas, though, one could never be sure. If he decided to have one of his sullen, stubborn spells she could implore him to no avail.

After a little time had passed she tiptoed softly down the hall to listen at the closed library door. From inside she could hear Barnabas' sonorous voice as he read. She stood there for a while, and then, satisfied that nothing was amiss, she returned to the living room. The stranger from England kept his word in at least one respect. He brought Greta back to the living room within a reasonably short time. He bade Greta a warm goodnight and offered Margaret a mocking smile as she saw him to the door.

"I trust you do not think I'm being overly friendly with your daughter," he said. "She is such a lovely child; I am drawn to her." Margaret met his glance sternly. "She has lived a very sheltered life, Cousin Barnabas. I fear it would be all too easy for a man of the world such as yourself to confuse her."

"You need not worry on that score," he promised. And with a bow he stepped out into the fog and a moment later was lost to sight.

Margaret closed the door with a puzzled expression on her own face. Was she being unjust to her husband's distant cousin? Was Barnabas, after all, no more than a pleasant young man trying to be agreeable to an afflicted young woman? Was she being too severe in her judgment of him?

She so far reversed her original thinking that she was almost ready to accept him for the attractive young man he appeared to be. But her tolerant mood was shattered by a later shocking discovery. While she was helping a quietly happy Greta to bed she once again noticed those peculiar red marks on her daughter's throat. She knew they were fresh; they had not been in evidence earlier in the night. Once again she thought of witchcraft and her blood chilled. She determined to return to the old house at the first opportunity and tell Barnabas that he must leave Greta alone.

During the next several days the weather grew worse. The fog gave way to rain and then veered back to a heavy mist once again. Greta chafed at being restricted to the house. And for the first time Cousin Barnabas did not make his evening visit for several nights.

On the following Tuesday Clare Blandish arrived in the early evening with the little girl, Judith, in the carriage with her, along with a suitcase containing the child's belongings. She would be a guest at Collinwood for at least two weeks, Margaret having received, finally, Jonas' grudging consent. Margaret liked the little girl on sight, and Greta, welcoming Judith warmly, put aside the moping mood she'd been in since Barnabas had interrupted his visits.

Best of all Judith seemed to be happy with them. She stood by the pretty young widow and shyly asked, "Am I to stay here, Mrs. Blandish?" For a child she had an assured, pleasant voice.

Clare Blandish smiled. "For a short time at least. Don't you like Collinwood?"

"I believe I will," Judith said confidently, with a winning smile for Greta and Margaret. At once she went over to ply Greta with questions.

Margaret felt it was exactly what they needed to restore balance in the house. She was delighted to listen to Greta and the child chatting happily together. She and Clare relaxed to talk of village matters.

Then the young widow asked her, "What about your Cousin Barnabas? Is he still living in the old place?"

Margaret's face clouded and she glanced apprehensively in the direction of her daughter and the child, Judith, who were at the other end of the room. In a quiet voice, she said, "Yes. He is still here."

"Greta was so enthusiastic about him. I would like to meet him," Clare said.

Margaret hardly knew what to answer. So she solved the problem by changing the topic back to the new course her husband's business was taking, and how well the fishing boats were paying. She was still giving Clare details of this when the knock she had come to fear sounded on the front door. She knew even before she went to answer it that it would be Barnabas.

Barnabas was as charming as ever as he greeted her. And later when he was introduced to Clare Blandish and shook the hand of the pretty little Judith he was at his best.

As he kissed Greta's hand he told her how much he had missed her during the evenings when he'd been absent. He referred vaguely to a slight indisposition of the chest which had confined him to his room. Then, studying Judith as she stood shyly by Greta, he smiled delightedly.

Turning to Clare Blandish, he said, "Of course you were right. There is a most remarkable similarity in looks between these two. I vow that when Judith has grown to be a young woman she will have the identical beauty of dear Greta."

The young widow nodded with pleasure. "I saw that the first time I met Judith."

"And we both resemble Josette, whose portrait you admire so," Greta said happily.

Barnabas looked at the girl in the wheelchair thoughtfully. "That is true. It is a remarkable situation. A kind of double coincidence."

For the balance of the evening he was the key figure. And when Clare Blandish, who was plainly taken by the Englishman's charm and fine manners, at last said she must leave, he insisted on seeing her to her carriage. Although Margaret was at once uneasy for her friend she was relieved to so easily be rid of Barnabas. Greta did not seem to notice her admirer's sudden switch in interest to the young widow since she was busily engaged in entertaining Judith.

Once again Barnabas was absent for a week. And when he did present himself one lovely July evening, Clare Blandish was on his arm. It was dark and Clare spoke of Barnabas having met her at her home just after dusk had settled. She seemed in the same ecstatic, dreamy mood Margaret had so often seen her daughter in while under the stranger's influence.

Margaret was further alarmed by remarks that indicated Barnabas had been visiting Clare regularly and had been introduced to her charges. He discussed the excellent work Clare was doing with the orphanage and soon had Judith seated on his knee while he answered her questions about what it was like to sail on the ocean. And once again he seemed to be able to repair his neglect of Greta with a kiss for her hand and a few earnest words of apology.

"My work," he told her. "Each day the demands become greater on me."

"I have missed you so," Greta told him with wide-eyed sadness.

Barnabas patted her hand. "I will make up for those lost evenings, I promise you."

Margaret took in this scene with misgivings. While she had not meant to involve Clare with him, she was glad that he was less persistent in his attentions to her daughter. And as she turned to speak to the young widow she found herself staring at her throat. For around it Clare was wearing a scarf of some filmy material, a thing she had never done before to Margaret's knowledge.

"Barnabas has had many excellent suggestions about improving the treatment of my orphans," the young widow said with a pleased smile, and as she spoke her hand went up to touch her throat—at those exact places where Margaret would expect the weird red abrasions to be!

Margaret had a strong urge to tear the scarf from her friend's throat, to satisfy her suspicion that it concealed those telltale scars. But she did not dare to do so. And new alarm swept through her as she heard Barnabas assure her daughter that he would be around the following evening to take her for a tour of the garden in the moonlight.

"The weather is much better now," he was saying. "I'm sure it will do you good."

"I know it will," Greta replied enthusiastically. "I've missed our walks."

Margaret turned to them with a forced smile. "You mustn't be greedy, dear," she chided Greta. "You have Judith for company now. Barnabas is right in dividing his scant free time with Clare."

Barnabas merely showed a tolerant smile on his handsome, hollow-cheeked face in response to this. And before leaving with Clare he took Judith up in his arms to the child's squealing delight. It was all very warming except that Margaret didn't believe any of it. She was now convinced that this cousin from England was playing a part, that he was something quite different from what he pretended. And whatever the truth might be, she felt it must have macabre overtones.

Clare smiled at her nervously as she hesitated at the door before going out into the darkness with Barnabas. She said, "It is very good of you to take such an interest in Judith. Barnabas thinks the child is lovely. He's even spoken to me of adopting her."

Margaret found this more alarming news. Trying not to show her concern, she said, "But surely Barnabas would find a child somewhat of a burden when he returns to the busy outside world?"

Barnabas answered for himself, "Judith would never be a burden to me. But I hesitate because I'm dubious about Hare's ability to adjust to the youngster."

They said goodnight then and left. When Margaret returned to the living room Greta and little Judith were talking and laughing. They seemed to find great happiness in being together. And she made a vow not to let anything destroy that happiness.

The next morning when Ada came upstairs to do the rooms Margaret took her aside and in a low voice asked her, "What about Patience?"

Ada looked frightened. "It's just the same, ma'am."

Margaret stared at her. "You mean she is still getting up in the middle of the night to meet Barnabas Collins?"

"Yes. Almost every night. And those marks still show on her throat. I don't think she is well," Ada went on worriedly. "She is getting miserable thin."

"I must have a talk with her," Margaret decided. And she went downstairs to seek the girl out at once. She found her in the kitchen working while Granny Entwhistle sat in her usual chair by the enormous cooking stove with its array of great pots and pans.

To make her mission less obvious Margaret first addressed the old woman. "How is your arthritis today, Granny?"

Granny's wrinkled face showed resignation. "I can suffer my body pains," the old woman said in her thin, high voice. "It is the black suffering of the soul that torments me."

Margaret frowned. "You should have no qualms of the soul, Granny. You have always been a fine woman."

"Sin and the Devil have come to Collinwood again," Granny intoned. "I can fair smell the evil around me."

"What sort of evil?" Margaret asked sharply.

"Last night a giant bat beat its wings against my window," Granny said. "And I knew it had come to steal my soul. To suck my blood and destroy my spirit."

"You mustn't imagine such things, Granny," she told the old woman. "You are only making yourself miserable." And she quickly walked away from her, shaken.

She approached Patience who was peeling and slicing apples. It seemed to her the girl tensed as she moved close to her. Ada had been right in saying Patience was looking thin and pale. A waxen pallor had come to her cheeks and her bare arms had the same unhealthy appearance. Margaret asked her, "Are you feeling well, Patience?"

The girl smiled nervously. "Very well, ma'am."

"You don't look it," she told her. "You look as if you needed both rest and nourishment." She eyed the girl sharply. "Do you get lots of rest?"

"Yes, ma'am." The girl looked away to concentrate on the peeling of the apples.

Margaret said, "I have heard a different story. It has come to my attention that you waken almost every night and leave your room to meet the newcomer who has rented the other house."

Patience turned to her with consternation written on her pretty face. "But you can't believe that!"

Margaret's eyes had moved to the girl's throat and two familiar dull red spots. "What are those marks on your throat?"

The maid touched a hand to them defensively. "I don't know. It is a rash that has plagued me. It comes and goes."

"Then you deny ever leaving your bed to meet Barnabas Collins?" Margaret asked in a tone too low to be heard by Granny, dozing at the other side of the big stone-floored kitchen.

"Indeed I do, ma'am," Patience protested. "Whoever told you such a thing should be ashamed! Do you take me for a hussy?"

"No, I don't, Patience," Margaret said wearily, sensing that the girl's indignation was sincere, that she knew nothing of her midnight sorties.

"If I thought you doubted me, ma'am, I'd leave your service," Patience went on unhappily.

"It's all right. I'm sure it was a mistake. Think nothing more about it," Margaret told her. "And do take better care of your health." With that she left the girl.

Not until she was alone in the hallway did she fully realize what Patience's reply to her question meant. It left her no alternative but to confront Barnabas with her findings and let him know she believed him to be a threat to their pleasant way of life at Collinwood. She would demand that he leave at once and hope that he would agree to do so. Her threat to involve her husband in sending him away would be an idle one. She knew she could not count on Jonas for any support.

But she also knew that she must rid them of Barnabas Collins. She had not quite decided the kind of peril he represented. But she felt it was a real one for Greta and the child Judith, not to mention Patience or Clare Blandish who seemed to have fallen as readily under his hypnotic charm as the others.

Perhaps Granny was right, and the handsome, gaunt cousin from England was somehow linked with the powers of evil. Barnabas might have returned to Collinwood to do the Devil's bidding. Yet he had done no more than terrify her thus far and she was the only logical adversary to challenge him.

The entries in the ancient journal still haunted her. The dead Parson Collins had hinted of a strange evil which had taken over the old house in that long ago day. He had written of witchcraft and Granny Entwhistle had connected him with a certain Angelique, whom she had called a witch. Margaret wished she had been able to find more on the subject. But death had stopped Parson Collins' investigation.

These thoughts made her wonder if Parson Collins was buried on the estate. And what about the original Barnabas? As far as she knew he had never returned. But if he had, his gravestone should mark his last resting place in the cemetery. Perhaps the witch, Angelique, was also buried there! She decided to make a quick visit to the cemetery after the evening meal and check the various monuments. And on the way back she would stop by the old house and tell Barnabas Collins what was on her mind.

Greta was in a cheerful, eager mood that evening. She insisted that her mother bring out a blue dress that set off her blonde beauty. And she took extra care in arranging her generous tresses. All the while, Judith stood by in silent admiration. The little girl had formed a strong attachment for the invalid.

Margaret helped her daughter, knowing full well the reason for these urgent preparations was the promised visit of Cousin

Barnabas. And though Margaret intended to prevent the visit if it was within her power, she went along with the preparations.

As soon as dinner was over Margaret left Greta and the little girl in the company of Jonas while she slipped out the rear door of Collinwood. It was a warm lovely July evening with the sun just beginning to set. She made her way across the yard quickly, a slim, elegant figure in a full-skirted beige dress. If possible, she wanted to carry out her errands before she was missed in the house.

Taking a different path, she avoided the old house and first went directly to the cemetery. The iron-fenced square of graves on the edge of the forest looked less grim in the warm red rays of the setting sun. The rows of granite stones, crosses and pillars reflected the crimson glare of the dying sun in a quite fantastic manner. As she moved from one neat grass-covered mound to another her shadow came between the rays of the sun and the monuments and she was able to read their inscriptions.

Suddenly she found herself in front of a worn stone of red marble on which was the barely decipherable name: "Josette." Her heart leaped. Could this be the Josette? She knelt to study the stone further and try and see the dates inscribed on it. But it was useless. Too many years had passed; too many storms had battered against it. The marble had dissolved before soft summer rain, the delicately shaped snowflakes of winter and the corrupting kiss of fog.

She was still on her knees by the side of this Josette's grave when she heard the rustle in the trees high above her. It was not like the normal sighing of the wind through the tall evergreens that stood like austere sentinels just beyond the small cemetery. Instinctively she raised her eyes from the worn lettering on the red stone to the point the sound had come from.

Peering up at the trees she finally saw a quick darting movement. And as she continued to stare a terrifying thing happened. From the covering branches of a majestic pine a huge bat came flying out. It was as large as the one that had broken her window. For a moment Margaret was too paralyzed with horror to move. Then, with a sharp cry of fear, she raised her hands to protect her head.

The bat came swooping down toward her, so close she could feel the motion of it. Scrambling away from the grave, she screamed again and ran from the cemetery. Again the giant bat came driving towards her. She beat out frantically with her hands and actually brushed the membrane of its wings for a fleeting second. Continuing to race forward, she sobbed out her terror.

And then, before she was halfway across the open field, it suddenly vanished. When she realized she was no longer in danger she stopped running and stood staring up into the air around her in wonder. It had gone as suddenly as it had appeared . . . almost as if its mission had been to frighten her away from the grave.

The experience had ended any hope of her exploring the cemetery further at this time. And it made her uncertain whether she was prepared to have a showdown with the sinister Barnabas. Yet this had to be done; Greta was waiting for his arrival even at this moment. If she hoped to save her daughter from his evil spell she had to go through with her plan.

She made her way slowly toward the old house, which looked as deserted and eerie as ever. The sun was finally sinking and a certain bleakness had come to the night on the edge of dusk. As she stared at the gray old building she decided she might use the same cellar entrance which had served her the previous visit. Providing, of course, it had not been padlocked again.

When she came to the door, which was flat with the ground, she saw the lock had not been restored to it. All she had to do was lift up one of the wooden sides and make her way down the stone steps. This time she was more familiar with the area. She let the wooden door close gently above her and then cautiously advanced down the steps into the cellar.

As soon as she reached the earthen floor she made a discovery. The panel to the secret room was open. She could see the glow of the lit candles emerging uncannily from the room.

CHAPTER 6

Pressing close to the damp stone wall of the cellar, she stared through the gloom at the soft flickering glow of candlelight beyond the narrow entrance. After a moment of breathless waiting and hearing no sound she found the courage to start slowly toward the room. At last she was in the entranceway and within a dozen feet of the closed oak coffin on the stand in the far corner of it. The candles, burned almost to the holders, were set out on a sideboard beyond the coffin.

As she nervously approached the massive coffin with its heavy ornamental bronze handles along the side she could notice no identifying plate on it. For all she knew it might have rested there in that cold, gray room for a hundred years! But someone was interested in it enough to keep those candles alight. She had seen Hare entering the room to take care of some chore, and no doubt it was the ugly deaf-mute who had left the secret panel open now.

Margaret was now close enough to touch the shining surface of the coffin's top. She stood there in the eerie glow of the candles with a look of perplexed fear on her attractive face. Did this coffin have a role in the experiments Barnabas had spoken about? Had he brought it with him or had he returned to Collinwood because he knew it was there? She did not dare to attempt a guess.

She turned to cast her eyes around the secret room. Its walls were of gray stone and, except for the coffin and the sideboard with the candles, it was empty. There were no windows to light its bleakness. In most respects it was a tomb. It had the odor of having been shut off for a long period. And staring at the casket again, she began to wonder if the body of a Collins lay in it. The strangeness of the atmosphere made her temporarily forget her danger.

All at once she was aware of the hazard of being there. She turned and started across the stone floor to the exit when a door slammed overhead and she heard heavy footsteps on the wooden stairs leading down to the cellar. She halted where she was, an expression of sheer panic spreading across her lovely face. It could only be Hare on his way back to the secret room! She was trapped!

She darted a glance around the room; there was no place to hide. In a moment Hare would be blocking the single exit. But it was too late to think about making a dash for it now. She had waited too long.

Then something happened that froze her with a new horror and made her forget about Hare. The lid of the coffin was rising! Very slowly, the shining oak top of the ornate casket was lifted, and when it had opened six or seven inches she saw a pasty-colored clawlike hand grope out from the dark crevice.

Too terrified to move or scream, she stood there like someone in a trance. Wide-eyed with fear, she watched the hand grasp the side of the casket firmly and only then did she recognize the black-stoned ring she had seen so often on Barnabas Collins' hand. The coffin lid was opened wide now and slowly a figure sat up in it. It was Barnabas, complete with the Inverness cape. As he reached sitting position he turned her way. The sunken eyes in the handsome, cadaverous face studied her with an amazement that equaled her own.

They might have stared at each other in silence for long minutes had not the eerie spell been broken by the sound of an angry, animal growl from the entranceway. Without turning, Margaret knew it had to be Hare. She was caught between this double horror and too shocked to make any attempt to save herself.

Hare came forward and grasped her roughly by the arm. He glowered at her and she could smell the heavy whiskey fumes on his breath. His hands bit into her flesh. At last she gave way to her terror, screaming shrilly. She pounded at the leering, bearded face with her free fist but it did no good. Hare neatly caught that arm as well.

Then Barnabas was between them. His gaunt face dark with anger, he grasped the startled Hare by the shoulder and with a strength she felt must have a supernatural basis hurled the bully back and away from her. After which Barnabas stalked his shocked servant, fixing his hypnotic eyes on him and making him cower and back out of the room. As soon as he vanished Barnabas turned to stare coldly at her.

"Why did you have to mix up in this?"

Margaret was feeling weak and nauseated, afraid she might faint any second. Somehow she collected herself enough to say, "I had to see you." Her voice was thin and tremulous.

"Now you have found me, are you any better off?"

She stared at him and then at the coffin. Her eyes sought him again. "What does it mean?"

"I should think you could guess. A smart woman like yourself," he sneered.

Her brain reeling, she recalled the sinister hints in the journal, the weird warnings of Granny Entwhistle, the giant bat— and those marks on the throats of the young women Barnabas had interested himself in. Didn't it all add up to something too horrible to believe?

She gasped. "You're not . . . human, are you?"

He smiled, but it was not a pleasant smile. "What a superior brain you must have to guess that!"

"But it can't be!" she protested, not wanting to believe it. "You're not—"

She didn't finish her question. It didn't bear finishing.

The look of hatred on the handsome, gaunt face was replaced by an expression of utter weariness. Leaning on the black cane with its silver wolf's head, he nodded slowly. "Yes. I'm the original Barnabas Collins. Dead for a century."

The enormity of it was still too much for her. "But you're alive and talking to me now."

"Because darkness has come," he said quietly. "I live in the hours from dusk to dawn. And then I come back to this." He indicated the coffin by pointing his cane at it.

"I've heard legends about such things," Margaret stammered weakly. "But I have never really believed them."

"You would do well to." The deep-set eyes were fastened on hers once more.

"Are you telling me that you are one of the living dead? A vampire who must feast on human blood to avoid the grave?"

"I bear that curse," the man in the caped coat said sadly. "I wanted to keep the truth from you. From everyone. That is why I rented this house where I was born. With Hare to protect me it seemed that I might rest safely here for a while."

"But you are mad!" she gasped. "You must be to try and make me believe such a story."

"I wanted to spare you the truth," Barnabas reminded her,

his tone becoming harsh again. "But you would not curb your female curiosity. Would not let me enjoy this sanctuary from the turmoil of the great world outside! I have wandered for a century and I must have rest!"

Margaret found it easier to believe he was mad or she was having a nightmare than to accept the story he was offering her. She said, "If what you say is so! If you are a vampire, then no one is safe here!"

Barnabas smiled coldly. "That is an exaggeration."

"But the girls! Even my daughter, Greta! Those marks on their throats! You have been drinking their blood!"

"My own survival depends on a daily quota of human blood," Barnabas told her calmly, the white teeth flashing as he spoke.

"You would weaken and perhaps kill my innocent invalid daughter," Margaret accused him.

"I am very fond of Greta," he said. "And I need not tell you she is in love with me. I have opened up her mind to new horizons since I came here. I have given her some hope."

"You have stolen her blood in the same way you did from the others. I have seen the marks on her throat," Margaret told him bitterly.

"But I have done her no real harm," Barnabas said. "On the contrary, I have brought her great happiness." His eyes took on an angry gleam. "And it would have been just as easy for me to kill her. As it would be easy for me to place you under hypnosis now and kill you if that was my desire." He paused. "I could bestow the kiss of death on you."

"What made you this way?" Margaret exclaimed in revulsion. "The kind of thing you are?"

Barnabas looked infinitely sad. "A woman's love and a woman's hatred. Often they become one and the same emotion. You have perhaps heard of Angelique?"

Margaret frowned. "She lived here long ago, didn't she?"

"She came here from the Indies. She was a witch. But I did not know that. Long before she arrived at Collinwood her soul had been poisoned by the voodoo rites of the island where she had lived. I was in love with Josette. You'll recall her portrait in the living room of the new house."

"The girl whom my Greta resembles?"

"Yes. That is what makes Greta someone special for me. And the child Judith as well, who also bears a youthful resemblance to my lost Josette. Seeing them here is almost like finding Josette again."

"What happened to Josette?"

"She killed herself. Threw herself over the cliff at Widow's Hill."

"Why?"

Barnabas bowed his head. "Because she had found out about me. What I had become."

"What had Angelique to do with it?"

The tall, handsome man lifted his eyes to meet hers again. "Angelique was in love with me. She tried to turn me against Josette. And she managed to convince me that Jeremiah Collins and Josette were in love, that Josette was betraying me behind my back. I challenged Jeremiah to a duel. Neither of us was severely wounded, but I learned that Angelique had been filling me with lies."

"What then?"

"I faced her with her villainy. And I was so enraged I made an attempt to kill her. I fired a pistol at her at short range. She thought she had been fatally shot and cursed me and any who loved me." He paused, a haggard expression shadowing his gaunt features. "A bat came flying at me from out of the darkness and bit me in the throat. She invoked it with her witchery. And I became one of the living dead from that moment on."

Margaret stared at him. "It's incredible. I believe you must be the great-grandson of that first Barnabas Collins. You must be touched by insanity!"

He shrugged. "If that will make it easier for you to accept me."

"What about the servant girl, Patience? She has been keeping a tryst with you every night."

Barnabas sighed. "I become very lonely here in the long night. If you will come upstairs with me I will show you how I try to solve that."

He gave her no choice in the matter, taking her by the arm so she could not make any attempt to escape him. His touch caused a cold chill to course through her. Slowly he led her up the rickety wooden steps to the ground floor.

Margaret meekly allowed him to lead her along the shadowed hallway of the ancient mansion, knowing well she had permitted herself to fall into the clutches of a madman—or something worse. It would be best to humor him and worry about getting away later on.

They arrived at the doorway of the living room and he took her in to view the table set for two which she had discovered on her last excursion. He pointed his cane at the table. "It's here that I dine each night with the lovely Patience. It is true I touch no food or drink but I see she is served the best by Hare and I find my enjoyment in sitting with her and feasting on her beauty."

"You take her from her bed to act out a mad charade here with you?" Margaret asked, staring at him.

He nodded. "I am, as I have said, an extremely lonely man. The interlude breaks the night for me. And it does the girl no harm."

"But it does!" she protested. "You spoil her rest and you take blood from her."

"She knows nothing of what goes on," Barnabas said evenly. "She is under my hypnotic spell. For her it is nothing but a pleasant dream." He lifted up the gown. "This was once my Josette's. When I see it on Patience I try to convince myself that she is my lost one."

"You're completely insane!"

He smiled bitterly. "As I understand it, most lovers are. It is tragic that your Greta is so deformed for she really could play the role of Josette to perfection. We could perhaps be married!"

Margaret's eyebrows lifted. "Do you think I would allow that?"

"I would be a devoted husband and Greta already is in love with me," he said. "But she is an invalid and so I will not press the matter. I wish only to offer her some love and hope. Now, with the child, Judith, it is rather different. Ten years from now she will be a reincarnation of my Josette. A beauty in full bloom."

Despite her fears Margaret gave him a scornful glance. "Much benefit that will do you!"

Barnabas showed a smile on his hollow-cheeked face. "Don't jump to conclusions, Cousin Margaret."

"I am not your cousin," she said defiantly.

He linked his cane over the chair back and took her gently by the arms, his deep-set black eyes drilling into her. "Do you not realize you are the kind of woman I could love if things were not as they are?" he asked in a taut voice. "You have beauty, strength of character and a kind heart. Virtues I admire greatly."

Margaret tried to avoid those hypnotic eyes, fearful of his overpowering her with his strong will. She, who had so long been the victim of a loveless marriage, was only too aware of the magnetism of this odd but handsome man. She trembled with the passion his words aroused in her along with the chilling fear she had come to feel for him. "Please, let me go!" she whispered.

He did. "You need not be afraid," he said in his suave fashion. "I mean you no ill so long as you do not betray me."

She took a step back from him. "What do you mean by betrayal?"

Barnabas smiled. "Do sit down. What I have to say will take a few minutes."

Margaret hesitated. She had no desire to remain there and only hoped he would allow her to leave. One could never tell with a madman. Yet she was curious to find out more about him and what was going on in the old mansion. And for that reason she was inclined to stay.

She said, "They will miss me at the house."

"I won't keep you that long," Barnabas said persuasively as he drew out one of the chairs at the table for her.

"Please say whatever you have to say," Margaret said, seating herself stiffly in the chair. "My daughter will be wondering where I am."

Barnabas smiled mockingly. "I will make it right when I visit Greta tonight. I'll tell her we met and went for a walk."

She looked up at him and said firmly, "I will not allow you to see my daughter again."

He studied her with mild surprise. "Greta is expecting me. She will be most unhappy if I do not come."

"I don't care about that," Margaret said. "After what I've seen tonight and the monstrous story you've told me, I do not want you near my child."

He sighed. "We'll see." At that moment Hare appeared in the doorway of the living room. He eyed Margaret with cool disdain and then gave his attention to his master. Barnabas gave him a quick signal and said, "Wine for the lady."

Hare either understood the gesture or read Barnabas' lips, for he at once went to the big sideboard and poured a glass of sherry, which he brought over and placed on the table before her. Barnabas gave him a nod and Hare left the room.

"I do not need the wine," Margaret said, although the truth was she felt a stimulant would do her good.

"I suggest you take it," Barnabas said with quiet authority. "I promise you it will do you no harm. It is the purest of fine old sherry."

Hesitantly she touched it to her lips. He was right. It was good sherry. She took a sip and felt it warm her as it went down. Still holding the glass, she asked him, "What was it you wanted to tell me?"

He had retrieved his cane and now held it crosswise in his two hands as he studied her thoughtfully. "Let us return to the subject of the child, Judith, again."

"I see no point in that."

He frowned. "But I do," he said. "Although she is only a child of nine she already bears a startling resemblance to my lost Josette."

"A resemblance mostly imagined on your part."

"No. Our mutual friend, Clare Blandish, was quick to note that she looked like your daughter. And in turn Josette. So we need not argue that point."

Margaret lifted her chin. "You have caught Clare up in the evil web of your charm," she accused him.

He smiled wanly. "Do you think so? I hope I have. Because that is rather important to my plan."

"What plan?"

"To adopt Judith."

It was fortunate she had drained the last of the sherry or she might have spilled it as she awkwardly returned the glass to the table. Her eyes were wide with surprise as she sat there staring up at him. "You can't mean it! You must be joking!"

He shook his head. "No. I'm quite serious. In ten years little Judith could become my bride. In the interim I'll see she has the life of a rich man's daughter. Every luxury and advantage will be given to her. So in the end she will be the same great lady Josette was."

"You can cold-bloodedly plan to marry that infant?"

"She will be a young lady in ten years. And that much time is really nothing to me," Barnabas went on confidently. "She shall first be my daughter and then my wife."

"That is absurd!" Margaret protested.

"Not at all," he said. "I'm positive Clare will arrange the adoption for me. And you and Greta can help me raise the youngster. I shall remain at Collinwood as the lovely child becomes a still lovelier young woman."

Margaret rose from the chair. "I warn you. I'll do everything I can to stop this."

"Why?" he asked, his easy mood changing.

"It is too cold-bloodedly cruel. You are mad. I will not see an innocent little girl offered as the victim for an insane lust."

Barnabas regarded her solemnly. "You are making a serious accusation."

"And I mean what I say!"

"Since it is to be a time for frankness," he said, advancing to her with an air of menace, "let me tell you a few truths. Number one, if I so wished you would not leave this house alive. Your body would be found on the beach and you would be written off as another suicide."

Her fears began to rise again. "You wouldn't dare."

"You don't think that," he said with the same cold menace. "I see the fear in your eyes. And you are wise to fear me since I am desperate. Not only do I ask your silence about what you have seen here tonight but I will expect you to actively assist me in the adoption of Judith."

"Never!"

He reached out and caught her roughly with his right hand. "Listen to me! If you do as I ask I will give you my guarantee that no harm will come to Greta. I'll offer her help and affection. She needs both."

"You want to bribe me by being kind to Greta! Do you think I'd trust you?"

His strong fingers tightened on her arm. "You had better," he warned her. "And I also promise the child shall not suffer. She will be reared with love and affection. Under my guidance she will become the ideal woman, and if at the end she does not love me she will be a most ungrateful creature."

"There is a good deal more to love than gratitude," Margaret told him.

"I'm not afraid to try the experiment," he said. "And it could mean all to me." He said this with such great passion she was impressed.

Her brow furrowed. "Why do you say that?"

"Because it is true," he told her. "I believe this kind of love and devotion could bring me back to a normal way of life."

"Cure your insanity? I doubt it!"

"There is more than insanity, whether you wish to face it or not," Barnabas warned her. "You could be helping save my immortal soul. Doesn't that strike you as being of importance?"

"For all your fine promises you go on deluding these poor girls," Margaret said. "Placing them under hypnotic spells and ravishing their throats. I cannot sanction such actions."

"I've given you my word that Greta and the child will be safe!"

She met his pleading eyes. "But what about Patience? And Clare Blandish? Or any other unfortunate girl who happens to fall under your power? Are you making promises for them as well?"

His lips worked nervously as he hesitated over a reply. The hand around her arm did not relent its grip. Frowning, he said, "I have to survive somehow until the spell is broken."

"And you think the love of this child will break it? Cure your madness?"

He smiled coldly. "I believe love is as good an antidote for madness as anything."

"My arm is numb; let go!" she gasped.

He let her go and, leaning his weight on the silver-headed cane, asked, "Well, what is your decision?"

"I have made none."

"I will assume you have decided in my favor," Barnabas told her. "Silence and the small cooperation I have asked will not put you out too much."

"It is late," she said tonelessly. "I must leave."

He stood there facing her in the candlelit room with his deep-set eyes regarding her solemnly. "I will let you go. I will let you go because I believe you will do what I say."

"I have made no promises," she warned him.

"I require none," he said. "Only remember, if you fail me my vengeance can be cruel. And it will fall not only on you but on your daughter." He escorted her to the front door. "I advise you to use this entrance in the future," he said in his mocking fashion. "I shall make certain the cellar door is properly secured. And remember, I am not to be disturbed in the daylight hours."

He opened the door and let her step out into the refreshing night air. She had no idea how much time had passed but it was completely dark now with a myriad of stars overhead. She heard the door slam behind her and turned to look at the grim old house, seemingly without a light. Shivering, she set out for Collinwood.

Somehow she had to protect Greta and the child from this madman. Yet, was he mad? He had argued sanely enough. Could there be such a curse? A curse which would turn a young man into a bloodsucking demon and let him wander the world in darkness for a century? Was Barnabas to be pitied rather than reviled? Should she try to help him as he'd begged her? Was this beyond her understanding, a mystery she should not try to solve but merely endure?

There was no one she could look to for advice. Jonas would declare her mad if she brought the story to him. Greta was under the stranger's spell and so was her closest friend Clare Blandish. So she was left to face this completely alone!

When she entered the house she went directly to the living room and found Greta alone there in her wheelchair and near tears. "Wherever have you been, Mother?" she asked. "It got so late I had to send Judith upstairs to bed with Ada."

"I went for a long walk," she said awkwardly. "I didn't realize it would take me such a time to get back."

"I've been imagining all sorts of dreadful things had happened to you," Greta went on. "And Cousin Barnabas hasn't come yet!"

Margaret tried to keep her face and voice expressionless. "Perhaps he won't come," she said. "It might be better if he doesn't."

Greta stared at her wide-eyed. "How can you say that, when you know his coming means so much to me?"

"You'll forget about him."

"Never!"

"That's nonsense!"

"It's not," she protested. "Since Cousin Barnabas has come here I've begun to hope to find some enjoyment in life. He's the first one to stop me from feeling like an ugly maimed little animal. Before he came I didn't want to live!"

Margaret studied her daughter's tormented face with alarm. Greta clearly meant what she was saying. Had they so failed her that this stranger had completely won her heart? Admitting that Barnabas was charming and sympathetic when he liked, still it seemed strange he could have gained such power over her daughter in such a short time. Of course hypnotism had played a role in it. But surely a minor role in Greta's case.

She said, "Then you have great confidence in Cousin Barnabas?"

"I believe he is a fine man," Greta said with shining eyes.

Margaret wished she could tell her bluntly what she had seen and been told in the old house. But she feared it would shock the girl into a state of apathy. She recalled all too well how the frail girl had sat with dull eyes in her wheelchair before Barnabas arrived. The hopelessness that had been all too evident in her despite her beauty and courage. And how changed that was now! Was she willing to pay the price for her daughter's continued happiness?

Her deliberations were interrupted by a single knock on the front door. Greta gave her a happy glance that said she hoped it would be Cousin Barnabas at last. Margaret said nothing but slowly went to the door and opened it.

Barnabas stood there in his familiar caped coat. He offered her a warm smile as he stepped inside. "I'm sorry to be late," he said. There was a mocking gleam in his deep-set eyes.

She met his gaze without flinching. "We have been hoping you'd come," she said quietly. It was more than an answer—it was an admission she'd decided in his favor. She would keep silent and support him.

He nodded and passed her to go on in to Greta. And as she closed the door she noted his fleeting shadow on the foyer wall. For just a moment it looked like a giant bat in flight. Was it a grisly warning?

CHAPTER 7

B arnabas kept his word.

Although as attentive and charming with Greta as he had been before, and though he took her for the usual tour of the grounds before he left, there was no sign of the tiny red scars on her throat. Margaret was careful to notice this as she helped Greta get ready for the night.

When her daughter was safely in bed she smiled up at Margaret from her pillow. "It was a wonderful evening," she said. "And I think Cousin Barnabas is more content here. He seemed so at ease."

"That is a good sign," Margaret commented, wishing that she might feel the same easiness herself. She was weighed down with doubts and guilt, afraid she had gone too far in this bargain to ensure her daughter's happiness.

Her sleep was ridden with nightmares in which she found herself back in the cemetery with the bat attacking her. She wakened at one point with a sharp scream and sat up in bed staring into the darkness. From her window there came the dull bumping of some night creature against the glass. Perhaps a large June bug— or could it be a bat? She shuddered at the thought. And it was some time before she was relaxed enough to lay back down and close her eyes.

In the morning Jonas rebuked her for screaming in the night and waking him. He frowned at her from the head of the breakfast table. "I can't imagine why you have these nightmares," he said. "Do you lunch before retiring?"

"No," she said. "I didn't have anything last night." She wanted to tell him about her experiences in the cemetery and at the old house so badly that she had to bite her lower lip to restrain herself.

"You fill your head with a lot of idiotic fancies," he complained. "And then you have bad dreams as a result."

She would have liked to have told him that his Cousin Barnabas spent the days sleeping in that dark secret room in a coffin. It would have done her good to witness the consternation on his severe face. But to do that would be to break faith with Barnabas—and Jonas wouldn't believe her, anyway.

After her husband had left for his office at the docks she pondered over the problem as she sat at the table. Had she taken too great a risk in making this truce with the stranger from England? It was quite possible the forces of evil which had made him what he was could take control of him when they wished and urge him to evil deeds. If that happened, with her knowing what she did, she would feel herself partly to blame. Yet how could she deliberately endanger Greta by speaking out?

She must soon make a decision. The longer she kept silent the more she was bound to him. After she helped Greta dress and had her taken out to the garden by the devoted Luke Sinnot, Margaret went to the library again and consulted a number of musty leather-bound volumes in a search of information about vampires. She found little to help her beyond a mention of a mass-murderer in England who had made a fetish of biting his female victims on the throat. He was later apprehended and executed. Margaret closed the volume with a look of perplexity on her attractive face. She would not allow herself to believe such creatures as vampires existed. Nor did she believe that this Barnabas was the one whose portrait hung in the hall; she wouldn't accept this. Not that the alternative was more pleasant since it would indicate he was probably a madman like the one referred to in the ancient volume.

Her research was interrupted by the appearance of Judith. The flaxen-haired youngster was wearing a china-dress and held a skipping rope in her hand. She told Margaret, "An ugly monster chased me just now."

"Oh?" She frowned at the child.

Judith nodded solemnly. "I was playing by the old house and he came out and shook his fist at me. And when I didn't move he came running after me making funny groaning sounds!"

"That was Hare, the servant over there," Margaret explained carefully. "He has an ugly temper and is afraid you will disturb his master. So do not go over there in the daytime."

"Luke says he is in the employ of the Devil," the child went on with a grave expression. "And that he once came after him."

"Luke is bound to make too much of such things," she told the child. "If you'll just play in the garden here you'll have no troubles."

Judith, who so resembled her own Greta as a child, gazed at her with questioning eyes. "Am I to continue living here?"

Margaret smiled. "Do you think you would like that?"

The flaxen head nodded emphatically. "I would. I like you and Greta and Granny Entwhistle. And I think Cousin Barnabas would make a wonderful uncle."

"Do you really?"

"Yes," Judith said. "He is ever so nice, even if he does have that awful crazy Hare working for him!"

"I'm sure he'll be pleased to know you think so much of him," Margaret told the child.

"But why don't we ever see him during the day?"

Margaret sighed. "He is occupied with his work. He visits us when he can."

"Greta would like him for a husband." Judith smiled with childish innocence. "She says she is in love with him."

"You mustn't listen to such talk," Margaret said, making a mental note to warn her daughter not to confide so in the little girl.

"Will Greta get better and be able to leave that old wheelchair?" Judith asked, concern shadowing her pretty face.

Margaret was at a loss as to how to answer her for a moment. Then she said evasively, "No one can really predict that, Judith. It is in the hands of One more powerful than any of us."

And then she took the little girl out to the garden to join Greta. At the same time a plan was forming in her mind. When luncheon was over she went to the stable and asked the groom to get the small carriage ready. With Luke as driver she set out on an afternoon call to Clare Blandish—a call she felt could not be delayed.

Luke enjoyed being given the responsibility of driver. A happy smile showed on his unlined, strangely boyish face as he urged the bay toward town. Margaret watched him with a tender interest. She felt a deep sympathy for the retarded young man who was so slavishly devoted to the family and especially Greta.

As he drove she said to him, "I trust you are keeping away from the old house. We want no further trouble between you and that Hare. And keep Judith away from him too. If you see her playing there please bring her back."

Luke nodded, his face shadowing. "He is a devil and a grave-robber!"

Margaret was astounded. "Whatever do you mean by a grave-robber?"

Luke looked sullen. "I watched him from the forest. He didn't know I was there. But I saw him in the cemetery. And he went down into the big tomb where all the old ones are buried. And when he came back he had something in his hand."

"Are you sure of all this?" she asked sharply.

"Yes, ma'am," Luke assured her. "He had a handkerchief looped to carry things in and it was filled with something he'd taken from the tomb."

"I see," she said. "Have you told anyone else about this?"

"No, ma'am."

"Then don't," she begged him. "Not until I have had a chance to find out what it means."

This disturbing conversation was ended by their arrival at the big yellow mansion with white trim occupied by Clare Blandish. Margaret discovered her out on the rear lawn with a woman assistant and her dozen or so orphan charges. The children were engaged in a game of lawn croquet. Margaret got down from the carriage and instructed Luke to take it to a shady spot and wait for her.

Clare had seen her and was now crossing the lawn with a smile on her pretty face. "Margaret!" she exclaimed, greeting her with a kiss on the cheek. "What a pleasant surprise."

Margaret smiled faintly in return. "I wanted to have a serious talk with you and I thought it best to come here."

"Of course," Clare said, studying her with a concerned interest. "I trust nothing is wrong at Collinwood?"

"Not really," she said.

Clare looked relieved. "Then let us go to the rear sun-porch where we can relax and watch the children at the same time. I'll have some lemonade brought to us."

Not until they were comfortably seated in the wicker chairs of the porch and a maid had served the cool lemonade did Margaret tackle the problem which was uppermost in her mind.

Giving Clare a direct look, she asked, "Are you seeing Barnabas Collins as often as usual?"

The pretty dark-haired widow blushed. Putting her lemonade down on the table beside her, she said, "He visits me almost every evening. I find him a wonderful conversationalist and surprisingly well informed about Collinsport and its history."

"I'm sure he must be," Margaret said dryly. "Has he ever spoken to you about adopting Judith?"

Clare registered surprise. "Oh, then he's told you already. Yes, he did mention it casually several times, and only this morning his servant brought me a written request from him to legally adopt Judith."

Margaret's eyebrows rose. "Hare was here today?"

"This morning," Clare repeated. "As a matter of fact I have the letter here in my pocket." And she reached into a pocket of her crisp summer dress and produced a folded envelope. "I've read it several times. He has offered to give the child the best education available, a good home and to make her the sole beneficiary of his will. It is quite touching. Would you care to read it?" She offered her the letter.

"It's not necessary," Margaret said. "I knew he had some sort of plan in mind."

"You sound as if you don't approve," Clare suggested.

"I'm not sure that I do."

"But what a wonderful opportunity for little Judith," Clare said. "I think it's the best of luck he's become so interested in the child."

"But is he able to take on the responsibility of raising a little girl?" Margaret wondered. "He is so occupied with his experiments. And Hare is hardly the type to look after a child." She had to try to discourage Clare but at the same time not put Barnabas in a bad light. It needed to be handled with great tact.

Clare gave her a puzzled smile. "But a man of his means would surely hire a proper governess for the child. It should present no problem."

Margaret decided on a desperate gamble. She looked down at her hands clasped in her lap and pretended embarrassment. "The truth is, I've taken a great liking to Judith myself," she said. "She is so much like my own Greta was as a child. I was on the point of asking to adopt her."

The approach worked. She looked up to see a sympathetic smile cross her friend's face. "Of course! I should have thought of that! Well, it really is a situation. Perhaps you and Barnabas should settle it between you. I would be happy to have her in either of your homes."

She looked at the attractive widow earnestly. "Let me make a suggestion."

"Of course."

"Barnabas is so set on adopting the girl and so willing to make her his heir it would seem unwise to try and frustrate him in this."

"My own thoughts," Clare agreed.

"On the other hand," Margaret said, "I do not care to see the child condemned to live in that silent old house, even given the services of a competent governess. So why not consider a compromise?"

"Such as?"

"Allow Barnabas to adopt the child with the provision she shall be raised by me and live at Collinwood until she reaches maturity. In that way I can be assured she has the proper training and surroundings and also Greta and I will have the pleasure of her company."

Clare's face brightened. "It sounds an ideal arrangement to me," she said. "After all, Barnabas is right there on the same property and can visit with the youngster whenever he likes."

"That would be understood. He would be her legal guardian and enjoy all the privileges of one," Margaret said. It seemed to her she had managed the best solution to a problem that had been tormenting her. "Of course, you'll have to be the one to make him agree to this."

"I think I can," Clare said.

"It would be better if you presented it to him as your own plan," she went on. "I would not want him to get the idea I've interfered, even though I'm doing it in his behalf."

"Of course, I understand," Clare smiled. "He says in his note he is coming here around nine this evening to get my answer. And I'll outline an arrangement such as the one you have suggested."

"Thank you," Margaret said, rising. "Now I really must be getting back home."

Clare walked with her to the front door and then, as if suddenly remembering, said, "There is one other thing."

"Yes?"

"In the note he asks permission to have the child's name changed from Judith to Josette."

Margaret felt a wave of fear for the helpless youngster again. "I don't think that would be wise. You should refuse permission."

Clare raised her eyebrows. "You think it so important? I was prepared to let him name her Josette."

"It would be a shock to her," Margaret protested. "She has always felt herself a Judith. I think it would be unfair, a bad way to begin the new relationship."

"Perhaps you are right," Clare admitted. "Then I'll discourage him from that idea."

"Josette appears to be an obsession with him," Margaret warned, "and I'm not sure it's healthy. It was Greta's resemblance to Josette's portrait which first attracted him to her. And now he sees a likeness in the child."

Clare seemed prepared to forgive Barnabas anything and to have no suspicions about him. "He is a romantic," she said. "And he adores the family history. I'm sure that accounts for his odd interest in the portrait and the girl who sat for it so long ago."

Margaret gave her a searching glance, regretting that a high lace collar shielded her friend's throat. She was certain Clare's warm attitude towards Barnabas was mostly based on his hypnotic influence over her, and the red marks on her throat would underline this.

She warned her friend, "You must watch yourself with Barnabas. For all his charming ways he has a strong will. And I'm not sure he is right in everything he sets out to do."

Margaret relaxed a little on the return journey to Collinwood. She had at least made an effort to stop Barnabas from taking complete possession of the little girl, and yet she had not been forced to betray him. He could not hold that against her. He might be upset by not having it all his way, but she felt she could cope with his annoyance. His anger might be another matter.

She was reasonably certain she had won in this initial move. Clare would insist she have Judith at Collinwood even though Barnabas became the child's guardian. This would protect the youngster from the unhealthy atmosphere of the old house, and avoiding the name change was also important in balking the weird obsession concerning Josette.

It struck her that from now on she would be interminably involved in this struggle with the charming yet sinister Barnabas. She still could not be sure of her true feelings about him. But he was like a magician when it came to bolstering her invalid daughter's spirits. And as long as this miracle went on, she would strive to protect Barnabas while rendering him as harmless as possible.

Collinwood dozed under a sleepy summer afternoon heat. As they approached the big house overlooking the ocean there seemed to be no one moving about. She had Luke halt the carriage before the front door.

Before she got out she warned him again, "Do keep out of Hare's way and tell no one what you saw when you were in the cemetery."

Luke studied her with his blank face and said, "Yes, ma'am." But she knew he couldn't be entirely depended upon.

When she entered the cool, shadowed foyer of Collinwood she paused for a moment to study the portrait of the first Barnabas. It seemed to her that in a macabre fashion the painting changed expression from time to time. Now the face that gazed down at her wore a cold, resentful look, where before it had been grimly placid. With a sigh she turned from it, deciding she was imagining things.

She knew Greta would be having a late afternoon nap in her room at this time so did not disturb her. Instead she started upstairs to her own room. When she reached her landing a sudden impulse decided her to go on up and look in on Granny Entwhistle, who seldom went downstairs on hot days like this.

The door was ajar and the old woman was seated in her rocking chair. Margaret went in.

"How are you, Granny?" she asked.

The tiny old woman halted in her rocking and the sharp eyes in the nut-brown face fixed on her. "I'm well enough," she said. "But there are others here who are not."

Margaret crossed to sit on the edge of Granny's bed. "What do you mean by that?"

"I saw him in the moonlight last night," the old woman intoned. "He was crossing the yard. And his mouth dripped with blood!"

She caught her breath. "Saw who?"

"Barnabas! The evil one! Who else?" Granny's wrinkled face took on a knowing smile.

"You must have been dreaming," she said, sickened by the old woman's words.

"Old Joshua pretended he'd gone away," Granny went on, "and they told everyone he was in England. But he was in the cellar. They made a secret room for him to hide his shame."

"Who told you that?" Margaret asked sharply.

"My old mother," Granny said. "It was common gossip around the village. They whispered that Barnabas would never die. The curse wouldn't allow it! And now he is back! And the blood is on his lips!"

"You're rambling," Margaret warned her. "Don't say such things!"

The old woman's skinny hands clasped the arms of her rocking chair. "I know it is true," she declared. "I know Barnabas is back because I have seen the sapphire star!"

Margaret frowned. "The sapphire star?"

Granny nodded. "He gave it to the pretty little one. That Patience! Poor thing, she didn't know about it. I met her in the hallway and when I saw it around her neck, sparkling blue in the moonlight, I slipped it off. She was still under his spell and didn't even sense I was there. I let her go on to her room and I kept the pendant."

"Where did it come from?"

"The grave," Granny said with an odd look.

"The grave?"

"Yes. Old Joshua gave it to Josette. And it was buried with her. But now Barnabas has come back and robbed her grave."

"You must be mistaken," Margaret told her. "It's probably a pendant like the original one."

"I know that it is the sapphire star," Granny declared, raising herself from her chair with difficulty. Slowly she crept across the room, and opening a dresser drawer, fumbled in it for a moment. Then she turned and held up a shining blue stone on a golden chain. "You see!"

Margaret got up and crossed over to examine the pendant. It did look like an expensive piece of jewelry. And it also had the suggestion of age in its design. She said, "May I keep this for a short time?"

"No!" The old woman fairly snatched it from her. "It brings disaster and death. It bears a curse."

"Then why do you keep it?"

Granny turned to the dresser drawer again as she secreted the sapphire star in it. After a moment she closed the drawer and told Margaret, "It does not matter about me. I have lived too long."

Margaret was concerned chiefly because it fitted in with what Luke had told her about seeing Hare entering the family tomb and coming away with a good bit of loot. She told the old woman, "You had better not mention that jewelry to anyone else."

"What does it matter?" Granny asked. "No one listens to me."

Margaret paused by the door. "You really believe the Barnabas who is here now is the same Barnabas who lived here when the old house was first built?"

Granny looked smug. "He can never die," she said. "It is his curse. But he must have blood. No matter what the cost!"

And so she left the old woman standing there defiantly by the dresser. This was a new problem. If Granny repeated her story to anyone else she would soon rouse suspicions about Barnabas—suspicions that couldn't easily be settled. In her newly assumed role of his protector, it seemed she would have to tell him.

Barnabas did not come that night. Greta was crestfallen but said nothing. And when he came the following night he only spent a few minutes with the invalid and Judith before inviting Margaret out into the garden with him.

When they were alone under the stars, separated from the house by a high hedge, Barnabas confronted her angrily. "Why have you interfered?" he demanded.

"In what?" she asked innocently, although she knew well enough what he meant.

"You prevented Clare from giving me full control of Judith!"

She gazed up at the gaunt, handsome face now contorted with rage. "You have been allowed to adopt her, haven't you?"

"On your terms!"

"Better than to be refused," she told him. "I did it for your good. To ease your temptation. And you will still have the pleasure of a daughter."

He looked slightly less angry. "If you had asked me, I would have been willing to have you be her foster mother."

"Then you should be satisfied as things stand now."

"Hardly," he said, "when it is you who have called the tune."

"I don't think that is important," she said. "What does count is that this child be allowed to grow to a healthy young womanhood."

Barnabas offered her a cynical smile. "I fear my intentions are somewhat less noble."

Margaret looked up at him defiantly. "She may replace Josette in your heart, but she can never become Josette. You must know that!"

"I am not so sure," he said. "She can be my redemption and one day she will be my wife."

"For the present that had best be our secret," she said. "There is another more urgent matter I want to talk to you about."

"Oh?" He had lifted the cane with its silver wolf's head until it was at waist level. Now he nervously worked his fingers over its handle.

"You have seen Granny Entwhistle, the old woman who used to be housekeeper here?"

He nodded, his deep-set eyes fixed on her. "I know her."

"She saw you crossing the yard the other night, and she claims there was blood around your mouth. More than that, she talks wildly about the curse and what it did to you. And she has a sapphire which she claims was stolen from Josette's grave."

His expression became one of horror. "Josette's sapphire!" he whispered. "How could she have it?"

"She says you placed it on Patience's neck. She took it off her while she was still in a trance."

"Yes," he said hoarsely. "I put it on the girl's neck when she donned Josette's dress. I must have forgotten to remove it."

"The old woman has it now," Margaret warned him. "I tried to get her to give it to me. But she refused. She says it is cursed."

Barnabas looked stunned. "But I must have it back! I must!"

Margaret gave him a reproachful appraisal. "Why did you have Hare rob the family vault?"

He frowned. "Who told you that?"

"Never mind who. I know. What was your purpose?"

"I wanted the sapphire and some other things that belonged to Josette and were buried with her," he said.

"And now you see what it has led to?"

"It was an accident. I was anxious to get the girl back into the house before she was missed."

"And I have warned you about victimizing Patience," she went on. "But you've refused to listen."

Barnabas drew himself up to his full height, his gaunt face set in a stern mask. "You have no control over me," he told her. "I have been kind to you and your daughter. And in return I ask your allegiance. But you will be the one to obey, not me."

"And if I refuse?"

"There might be unpleasant consequences," he said. "I wish you'd remember that." And with a curt bow he stalked away to vanish into the darkness.

She no longer doubted Luke's story about the grave robbing. Barnabas had not even tried to deny it. In certain matters he was strangely without conscience. In his desperate struggle to survive he could be ruthless. Over the years he had obviously learned to let nothing stand in his way. Should she cross him she need not expect him to spare her.

These thoughts and others like them tortured her long after she'd retired for the night. Sleep eluded her as she turned restlessly beneath the crumpled bed sheets. The heat of the summer day seemed trapped in the room as she lay there listening to her husband's light snoring front the adjoining bedroom.

And then there came the crash of breaking glass followed by a frenzied scream from the floor above. There was a second scream and a third which merged with some thudding sounds.

CHAPTER 8

Margaret was out of bed and on her feet by the time her husband's angry cry at being awakened reached her ears. She hastily put on a dressing gown and hurried out of the room to the hallway. Jonas emerged from his doorway at the same moment, fumbling with the tie of his robe.

"What insanity is going on here?" he demanded in his usual stern fashion.

"I don't know," she told him without a glance as she went on toward the stairs.

And then she saw the huddled form near the bottom of the stairway that led from the attic floor. It took just a moment to discover it was poor old Granny Entwhistle. Clad only in the long flannel nightgown which was her night attire in all seasons, she lay there in a crumpled heap.

Others gathered around as Margaret knelt by the old woman's broken body—Ada and Patience, looking pale and frightened; Jonas staring blankly at the motionless figure.

"Well?" he demanded.

"She's dead," Margaret said. "I expect she stumbled at the top and fell all the way down."

"She's been especially vague lately," her husband said without a hint of sorrow in his voice. "No doubt she became confused and wandered out here."

Margaret's throat was tightened with sorrow and fear. "See her face!" she said in a whisper. "She looks as if she had been terrified by something."

"By falling down the stairs," Jonas said practically. "We'd better get her back up to her room."

The two maids stood by with Margaret as Jonas easily lifted the body of the dead housekeeper in his arms and mounted the steps with her. Margaret gave the girls a look and thought that Patience seemed in a distraught state. The pretty maid was ghastly white and trembling.

"I thought I heard another sound," she said. "What about you two?"

Patience seemed incapable of speech. She merely shook her head.

Ada spoke up. "I heard it too, ma'am. It was like the breaking of glass."

"Yes," Margaret agreed as she started up the stairs.

The maids followed her. Almost at once Patience hurried off along the upper hall to her own room. Ada told Margaret in a whisper, "She'd barely returned to her bed when it happened. The noise brought her out of her spell sudden-like."

"I guessed that," Margaret said in a low voice.

Jonas came out of the old woman's room to meet them in the hall with a puzzled frown on his stern face. "Odd," he said. "One of the large window panes is broken in there. As if a rock had been hurled through it."

"That must have been what frightened her," Margaret said, her own heart beating rapidly as she tried to appear calm.

"Could have been," her husband agreed, rubbing his chin in a disgruntled manner. "At any rate, it has ruined my night's sleep. And on top of that we'll have all the nuisance of a burial." With that, he angrily clumped downstairs.

Staring after him, Margaret felt disgust for his behavior. Over the years this husband of hers had gradually changed until now he was little more than an unpleasant stranger. His mad craze for money and restoring the Collins fortune had dominated him completely. It was only for Greta's sake that she stayed on at Collinwood.

Now she was faced with this new horror. She turned from the stairs and approached the old woman's room. She had no doubt in her mind about what had happened. Acting on her warning, Barnabas had visited the old housekeeper to reclaim the sapphire star. Entering the spartan little room, she saw that Jonas had at least arranged the body on the bed decently with a sheet pulled up over the head.

She went to the window. One full pane had been completely shattered; she recalled the night when the hideous batlike creature had broken its way into her room. Then she went over to the dresser where Granny Enthwhisle had put away the pendant. A thorough search of it failed to reveal the sapphire.

It was wet and miserable the next afternoon when Granny was buried in the servant's section of the Collins cemetery. Luke had toiled all morning digging the grave in a corner near the forest and the rotund minister from the village was there to read the service.

Margaret had refused to allow Greta to attend since she felt so bad, and in any event the long trek to the cemetery in the wet fog and drizzle might injure her delicate health. Patience had been delegated to remain at the house with her and Judith.

All the others of the household were present. Even Jonas had dragged himself away from his account books long enough to stand grimly by the grave. Margaret's eyes brimmed with tears of genuine sorrow in losing Granny Entwhistle mixed with tears of regret for the part she felt she had played in her death. Of course Barnabas was not present. But once she thought she saw a stirring in the pines that towered above the new grave. And just as the final words of the service were being read, Hare came to stand on the fringe of the little group and stare at the proceedings sullenly.

When it was over Margaret went back to the house. Greta was waiting in the living room to hear an account of what had happened. Margaret answered her questions in a preoccupied mood. She wondered if she could go on after this exhibition of cruel violence by Barnabas. And she waited for dusk, when he must surely put in an appearance.

He came at the usual time, offering the expected polite condolences before devoting himself to reading to Greta and Judith for more than an hour. Margaret bided her time until he was ready to leave. Then she followed him out into the fog and wet of the front steps.

He stood there nonchalantly. "Well?"

"Don't pretend," she told him. "I know!"

The gaunt face registered surprise. "Know what?"

"What you did to Granny Entwhistle!"

"I have no idea what you're talking about," he said, drawing his cape about him and restlessly prodding the step with his cane. "You should go back inside, you'll catch a cold out here."

"You killed her! And you took the sapphire!"

He stared at her. "What sapphire?"

"I shouldn't have told you about it," she said, her voice filled with remorse. "I might have known what you'd do."

"I don't remember you telling me anything," he said coldly.

"You have allowed the death of this unfortunate old woman to upset you unduly."

"Unfortunate old woman!" Margaret said bitterly. "Indeed she was! Why didn't you just take the pendant and let her live? No one would have believed her stories. She said that and she was right."

He touched her arm. "Don't distress yourself. The old woman fell downstairs and broke her neck. No one was to blame!"

"You were to blame," she said in a low, tense voice that wouldn't reach the others inside. "And so was I, in a way. You broke that window and made the attack on her! I remember the bat that came into my room the night you first arrived here."

"A distressing coincidence. I don't blame you for remembering it so vividly," Barnabas said. "But hardly a basis for the ridiculous accusation you made just now."

"All right," she said. "Deny it."

"I have no alternative."

"Perhaps not," she said. "But I warn you. One more killing and I will not keep your secret. Your night prowlings must stop short of murder or I refuse to protect you."

Barnabas made a great show of tolerance. "I'll not hold this against you," he assured her. "I know how upset you are."

"Just remember what I told you," she said.

His gaunt face took on a rather menacing smile that revealed his perfect white teeth. "I do not appreciate threats." And with a bow he left her and disappeared in the fog-shrouded night.

Only then was she conscious of the biting cold of the dampness. She shivered and went back inside. She hoped that he would believe her. And she further hoped it was in his power to obey her. For she had not been talking idly. Regardless of the sacrifices she was willing to make for her invalid daughter's security and happiness, she was not going to condone murder.

It was more than three years later before she had to face up to a similar crisis.

In the meantime Judith had grown from a child to a lovely and intelligent teenager. Barnabas had been accepted as her foster parent and Margaret had kept to her promise to rear the girl as a young woman of whom he could be proud.

Margaret felt the passage of time had mellowed the handsome, gaunt man. He had never ceased to show attention and kindness to Greta. And Margaret was pleased to note that her invalid daughter's dream of marrying Barnabas had been put aside for a gentler passion. Greta now seemed content to have the gaunt Englishman as her close friend.

Of course there was no question that Barnabas continued his weird nocturnal prowlings and kept to himself during the days. And Patience was still under his hypnotic spell although Margaret had noticed a new restlessness in the pretty maid in recent weeks. She continually worried about her and had pleaded with Barnabas to ease his hold on her whenever the opportunity presented itself. But it was one of the matters on which the gaunt, handsome man was unbending. He refused to even discuss it. Meanwhile, Margaret could see Patience fading in health. She had come to take on a wraithlike frailty which caused her to look older than her twenty-odd years.

Barnabas had been accepted by the village as a wealthy eccentric. He made rare visits to the Blue Whale Tavern but always kept to himself. He would take a place at the empty end of the bar and order a brandy, over which he would linger long before flipping a coin to the bartender and silently going his way.

Hare, except for two or three drunken spells, gave no trouble to anyone. Luke had learned to keep away from the old house and so avoid annoying the deaf and dumb man. Several times Margaret had wanted to visit Barnabas to discuss the raising of Judith, but memory of that secret room and the coffin in which he slept held her back.

Barnabas continued to visit Clare Blandish, who was busier than ever with her private orphanage. Things did not change much in the quiet fishing village, but one development was notable. The hard work which Jonas had put into his business was showing results. He was prospering and with his accumulating wealth he became less cold and severe with Margaret.

It was his custom to come home earlier in the day now and enjoy a glass or two of sherry before his dinner. He liked her and Greta to join him in the living room at this hour, when he would give them an account of the happenings at the plant and in the village.

On one such evening in May he spent some time telling them of an order he had received to ship salted cod to the West Indies. "It will mean doubling the fishing fleet," he said happily as he stood by the sideboard with his sherry glass in hand.

From her wheelchair Greta said, "That proves your theory that the future for the business is in fishing."

Jonas smiled at this. "I believe I possess a certain limited vision. Of course, we still have a large enough fleet of our own to take care of the shipments."

"And that should cut down on costs," Margaret suggested.

"It will be most helpful," he said, taking a sip of his sherry. He had put on some weight with late middle-age and gray side-whiskers added to his pompous appearance. "By the way, the village is greatly excited about an incident which took place last night."

"Really?" Margaret said, only mildly interested. She seldom

went into Collinsport unless it was to shop in the afternoons.

Her husband thrust a hand behind his back as he stood evenly balanced on both feet and nodded importantly. "A most unpleasant incident, I may say."

"Don't make such a mystery of it, Father," Greta pleaded. "Tell us what happened."

"It should serve as a warning to you both," Jonas Collins went on in his solemn way. "I have always advised you against going to the village after dark. And I believe this bears me out."

"Please get to the point, Jonas," Margaret said.

"Well," he said, relishing the attention he was being given, "as I heard it, one of the village girls was at the Blue Whale Tavern with her young man last night. They had a quarrel and she left on her own. She had to walk some distance to her home which is on the outskirts of town at this end of the main road. As she came to the section where there are few houses she heard footsteps behind her. Heavy footsteps following her!" He paused for effect.

Greta said, "Do go on, Father."

"She turned and saw a tall man dressed in black only a short distance away and coming after her. Becoming panicky, she screamed and began to run. Of course the man quickened his pace. She decided to try throwing him off the track by leaving the road and taking a shortcut that went by a gravel pit. For a time she thought she had eluded her pursuer."

"But she hadn't?" Margaret asked, beginning to worry a little. It struck her that the man in black could have been Barnabas. He'd behaved well enough for a long while but there was always the risk of his becoming violent.

"The whole thing becomes a little strange at this point," her husband told her, frowning at his empty glass. "According to the girl's story, she took refuge in the gravel pit, planning to hide there until the man chasing her had gone away. It was actually a stupid thing to do since she'd trapped herself by entering the pit. She was soon to discover this."

"Did the man follow her in there?" Greta prompted him as he hesitated.

Jonas looked skeptical. "No," he said. "But the girl claims that she'd only been in the gravel pit a moment when a huge bat-like thing came flying in after her. It went to her directly and attacked her. She fell to the floor of the pit and fought to keep the disgusting creature at bay. It bit her throat and she lost consciousness."

Margaret was sitting very straight in her chair now, her face deathly white. Trying to sound casual, she asked, "But the girl escaped with her life?"

"Obviously," Jonas said with a scowl. "Or I wouldn't be able to offer you her account of what happened. She regained consciousness a little later and made her way home. She was so weak and upset it was necessary to have the doctor for her."

"What did he think of it all?" Greta asked.

Jonas shrugged. "Naturally he was skeptical of some parts of the account. Yet he believed she had been chased by the stranger and had received a bad shock. And there were also two rather unusual red marks on her neck which more or less bore out her account of being bitten by some winged creature."

Margaret no longer felt any doubts. She wondered what had tormented Barnabas into his bold attack. She said, "No doubt the girl was in a state of hysteria. You cannot put too much weight to her story."

"You know how gullible the villagers are," her husband said. "They're now spreading wild theories the girl was attacked by a ghost bird. Too ridiculous!"

Lost in the storm of thoughts, Margaret heard little else her pompous husband said either then or at dinner afterward. And as soon as she could slip away from the house without attracting undue attention, she went quickly through the yard to visit Barnabas.

It was nearing dusk on the coolish, clear night as Margaret mounted the front steps and lifted the large brass knocker. After a moment she heard heavy footsteps coming along the hall. The door opened and Hare peered out at her in his surly fashion.

Hoping that the deaf-mute would be able to read her lips, she said, "I must see your master. It is most urgent!"

Hare continued to stare at her with a scowl on his ugly face. Then he stood back to allow her to enter. She went inside and was at once aware of the damp cold in the ancient house. She doubted that Barnabas ever bothered to use the fireplaces which were in almost every room. With a curt gesture, the servant indicated she should go into the living room. She did. The drapes were closed and the room was in darkness except for the faint light seeping in from the hallway. With the continuing approach of dusk it would soon be completely dark in there. She shivered.

Nothing had changed there in the three years since she'd been in it. The table for two was still set and ready. But most of the other furniture in the shadowed room was covered with shroudlike sheets. The tall grandfather clock in the corner was silent and its hands stilled. Time meant little to Barnabas.

She thought of Patience coming to this bleak room night after night under the gaunt man's hypnotic spell—no wonder the girl looked ill. The stench of stale air and mildew was overpowering. And the silence was unnatural and frightening.

The creak of a floorboard in the hall outside warned her that someone was coming near. She turned with a frightened look as Barnabas came through the doorway, an ominous figure as he stood there in the shadows in his caped coat with his familiar black cane in hand.

"Why have you come here?"

"I had to see you alone."

"I can't imagine why," he said harshly, the deep-set eyes flashing with anger.

She unflinchingly met his gaze even though she was secretly afraid. "You were in the village last night?"

"What about it?" he asked, too nonchalantly. "I stopped by the Blue Whale for a drink."

"I knew it!" she murmured.

The gaunt, handsome face showed a frown. "What are you suggesting?"

"The girl!" she said. "The one you followed and attacked last night. She's been telling the story around. Why did you do it?"

He rapped the cane with its silver wolf's head on the floor in an angry gesture. "I'll brook no such talk!"

"I know it's true," she said, not taking her eyes from him. "What made you do such a mad thing? After so long?"

"I tell you I know nothing about what happened to the girl!" he exclaimed as he took a step past her and stood with his profile to her, avoiding her accusing eyes. "Someone follows a village girl! Is that so unusual? And then later she is frightened by some large bird, after she's already so hysterical she's ready to imagine anything. Why should it have any bearing on me?"

"Because of the marks on her throat," Margaret said evenly. "You are the only one who leaves such marks!"

Barnabas whirled on her angrily. "You pretend to be my friend and yet you come here and say such things to me!"

"You must want to lose Judith," she said. "And with your plans so much nearer to fulfillment. She is growing up. In only a few years she will be old enough to think of marriage."

The anger drained from his sallow face to be replaced by a look of mild panic. "You can't take Judith from me," he said. "I am her guardian."

"I have only to tell what I know and you won't be!"

Barnabas smiled coldly. "You won't do that while Greta needs me. You still want happiness for your precious daughter and I'm the only one who can make her forget she's a helpless invalid."

"There are other ways," Margaret said, although her tone had already lost some of its resolve. "I can persuade Jonas to take us all on a long ocean voyage. And perhaps place Judith in a finishing school in France. I know of such a convent school attended by many young ladies from Boston."

The tall, handsome Barnabas quickly took on a different attitude. "You are judging me too hastily," he insisted. "Think this over and you will know you are wrong."

"I came here to warn you again," she said evenly. "There must be no more violence. I said that when Granny Entwhistle met her death three years ago. I meant it then as I mean it now."

"That old woman had an unfortunate accident," Barnabas said. "You shouldn't blame me. Nor should you hold me responsible for what happened to some village girl last night."

He would not admit his guilt; it was useless to continue the argument. Hastily she bade him goodnight and left. Something was driving Barnabas to seek new victims for his macabre needs. Until she knew the reason and how desperate he was, she would have no idea of what to expect. He called on them at Collinwood only about three times a week now. And she doubted if he would come by tonight, knowing how she was feeling about him.

Reaching the main house she went to the kitchen to find Ada working. She asked the girl where Patience was. Ada looked so upset by her question she continued with, "What is wrong?"

"I don't know what's come over her," Ada confessed, with a doleful air. "She's having one of her bad headaches again. She gets them frequent now. I told her I'd finish, and for her to go upstairs and rest."

"You did right," Margaret said.

"It must have to do with that Barnabas," Ada went on. "In the beginning she seemed so happy. And even though I worried about her going to meet him night after night I said nothing. Pretended I didn't know about it. But it has been different lately."

"How do you mean?" Margaret asked, thinking this might be a clue to why Barnabas had suddenly started to harass the village girls.

"I think she realizes what has been happening," Ada said, "though she hasn't said it out to me. And I think she's afraid of that Barnabas even though she still goes out to meet him most nights."

"I think I should talk to her."

"Don't tell her what I said," the girl begged.

"Don't worry."

Margaret went up the back stairs to the third floor and the bedroom the two maids shared. She discovered Patience stretched out on her bed in the almost-dark room, staring up into the shadows. When Margaret entered she sat up with a gasp.

Margaret crossed to her bedside. "It's all right, Patience. I know you came up here because you were feeling ill."

The pretty maid who had become so frail lately was quick to

get to her feet and awkwardly smooth her hair. "I'm all right now, ma'am," she said without conviction.

"I'm worried about you," Margaret insisted. "You haven't looked at all well lately."

Patience turned her back to her. "Perhaps I need a holiday," she said in a quiet voice. "It might do me good to get away from here."

"I think it might," Margaret agreed. "And now won't you tell me what has happened between you and Barnabas?"

The pretty girl wheeled around and stared at her in awe. "How did you guess?"

"I've guessed something was wrong for a long time."

Patience brought her hands up to her face and began to sob. Margaret put a comforting arm around her and after a moment or two the girl managed to get some control of herself. Blowing her nose and dabbing at her eyes, she turned an unhappy face to Margaret.

"It's only lately I've known," she said. "His power over me is fading. I was in a kind of trance but I'm not anymore. I remember the things he makes me do."

Margaret caught the note of restrained horror in the girl's tone. "You didn't realize you were meeting him at night in the beginning?"

"No. Not until a few months ago," Patience said with fear shadowing her face and voice. "One night I sort of came to and I was sitting at a table in the old house, wearing a strange sort of dress. There was food and drink on the table and he was sitting opposite watching me with those evil eyes."

"Does Barnabas know he can no longer fully hypnotize you?"

The girl nodded. "Yes. I told him. I hated him at first for what he had done to me. And then I realized I also loved him. I told him so. And I begged him to marry me and stop making me pretend I was this Josette he is always talking about."

Margaret sighed. "He refused, of course."

"He said he had other plans," the girl said bitterly. "I told him I would not go to him again. And for a few nights I didn't." The girl paused with a frightened glance Margaret's way. "And then I'd wake in the night and see him waiting down there. He always told me how lonely he was and how much my being with him meant. I still hoped he might change his mind about loving me, so I began meeting him again."

"But it is not the same?" Margaret suggested.

"Not for me and not for Barnabas either!" Patience said with misery in her tone. "Sometimes I cry or we quarrel. We have bitter quarrels. I don't know where it will end."

"You are right about leaving here," she said. "It is the proper thing to do."

Patience gave her a woeful look. "But I keep hoping Barnabas will change."

"Surely you understand what he is," Margaret said. "You must realize now there is no hope. Haven't you seen the marks on your throat on the mornings after your meetings with him?"

The girl sighed. "Yes," she said in a small voice. "In the beginning I didn't care. But now when he kisses my throat I feel as if my life were being drained out of me."

Margaret placed a comforting arm around the girl once again. "Don't fret anymore. I'll speak to Mr. Collins about finding a girl to replace you here. Then I'll see you have enough money to take a long rest a good distance from Collinsport. You must make up your mind to forget all about Barnabas and what has gone on here."

"Will he let me?" the girl asked.

"Leave that to me," Margaret told her.

Patience looked as if she might break into tears again. "He can be so good and kind when he likes. I'll always be in love with him!"

"He can also be the very soul of evil," Margaret warned her. "Once you're away from here you must put him completely out of your mind."

She left Patience resting and went downstairs. By the time she reached the first landing she could hear the voices below in the living room plainly. And she was somewhat surprised to recognize the suave tones of Barnabas among them.

And as she entered the living room a moment later she saw Barnabas standing by the fireplace with an arm fondly around the pretty Judith's shoulders as he finished telling the youngster and Greta a funny story.

Greta's appreciative laughter rang from the wheelchair as Margaret hesitated inside the doorway to watch the three. And Greta told the gaunt hero of her restricted life, "I don't know what I'd do without you, Cousin Barnabas. I'd pine away and die."

"We need never worry about that," Barnabas said with a smile. "For I plan to always remain at Collinwood." And he turned his eyes questioningly to Margaret. "Isn't that so?"

CHAPTER 9

The next morning brought a happening that swept all else from Margaret's mind. The day was sunny and warm and a little after ten Luke Sinnot came to the door to ask her if he might now take Greta out on the grounds. She gave him her permission and accompanied her invalid daughter as far as the garden, where the beds of tulips were bursting into bloom.

Greta studied the display of floral beauty with an ecstatic sigh. "Aren't they lovely?" she asked her mother.

Margaret smiled. "The gardener does well. And you help him, don't you, Luke?"

Luke, who had been wheeling Greta's chair, looked shyly pleased. "Yes, Ma'am."

Greta, whose beauty had been lately marred by a curious pallor, was wearing a rose dress that helped give her some color. She suddenly looked sad. "I wish Cousin Barnabas was here to admire the flowers with us. He sees them only at night. And that is no good at all."

"You must make allowances for Barnabas," Margaret said quietly. "He has his experiments to attend to during the day."

"But they seem to come to nothing!" Greta said with an almost childish petulance. "At least he never tells us anything about them. I can't imagine that they are so important."

Margaret could see that one day her daughter would demand to know the truth about Barnabas and his strange habits. The way things were shaping it could come soon. She was very much afraid Barnabas was headed for new violence and she would have to break her agreement with him. She could only hope that her daughter would not be too shocked when the revelation came.

She said, "I have warned you before, it is unwise of you to depend so much on Cousin Barnabas. In spite of what he tells you, things may change. He may leave here at short notice one day."

Greta looked up at her with amused incredulity. "There are moments when I feel you are trying to turn me against Cousin Barnabas."

Margaret had a difficult time hiding her confusion. She said, "Why should you think that?"

"The things you say," Greta told her. "The way I see you look at him sometimes, as if you feared and distrusted him. And I can't imagine why!"

"I have always taken a long while to feel a warmness to people," Margaret alibied. "Perhaps that is why I seem reserved where he is concerned."

"There is no use in attempting to disillusion me with Cousin Barnabas," Greta said. "I love him more than anyone."

Margaret was shocked by the girl's strong statement. "More than you do me or your father?"

Greta smiled. "The love I feel for both of you is quite different. But Barnabas sustains me. He is my life."

She was too troubled by her invalid daughter's words to continue the conversation. She said, "I must get back to the house. Judith is waiting for me to start her on her history lesson." She had undertaken the education of the girl personally and was finding great pleasure in it.

"The next time Cousin Barnabas comes, do please beg him to spend part of the days with us," Greta said. "We don't even see him every night lately."

"I'll mention it," she promised. "But don't count on his agreeing to it." And she left Luke to wheel the invalid on toward the cliff path.

When she returned to the house she paused to stare at the portrait of Barnabas in the foyer. Again the expression of the face in the painting seemed to have changed. In the bright morning sunshine the gaunt features had a look of extreme sadness. It was startling!

"Why are you so upset by the painting?" It was Judith who had come to stand by her and ask the question.

Margaret at once managed a thin smile for the youngster.

Judith was growing into a beauty and as her hair darkened slightly she came more to resemble Greta. "I'm not upset, really. I was thinking how much our Barnabas looks like the one in this portrait."

"And he says I'm almost a double for that Josette whose picture is in the living room. I think I look quite different! I'd rather be myself!"

Margaret laughed gently. "I think you are quite right. It is important to be yourself and be admired for your own beauty. All this dwelling on look-alikes is nonsense."

Judith brightened. "Do you think I'll be pretty on my very own?"

"Of course I do!" Margaret said. "You'll turn the heads of all the Collinsport young men. But you must also be intelligent. So now we'll go to the library and begin our history lesson."

She was in the library when she heard the first muffled shouts from the front lawn. She hurriedly got up and went out to see what was wrong. When she opened the front door Luke came racing towards her in tears.

"Miss Greta!" he cried. "Something's happened to her! She's gone all limp!"

Before he'd finished his words she was racing out across the lawn to where the wheelchair was. She prayed as she ran, hoping against hope that her daughter had merely fainted from the sun. But Greta never fainted.

When she came up to the chair and saw the limp body and the closed eyes of her invalid daughter she still hung on to the forlorn hope that it was nothing serious. But she soon knew better.

Greta's heart still showed a faint, erratic beat. At least she was alive. Somehow, with Luke's help, she got her back to the house and on the bed in her room. She summoned the groom and had him rush to the village for Dr. Grundy. In the meantime she began a vigil at the bedside of her unconscious child.

Dr. Grundy arrived first and Jonas, whom the groom had also summoned, came soon afterward. Dr. Grundy, a thin little man with steel-rimmed glasses and a perfectly bald head, was liked in the village and Margaret had a great deal of confidence in him. His examination of Greta took a considerable time. Then he joined her and Jonas in the living room.

"It is her heart," Dr. Grundy announced gravely. "She has had a rather severe attack but I have reason to hope she will recover from this one."

Jonas, for once, showed deep emotion. "From this one?" he asked in a broken voice. "Are you telling us there will be others?"

"You must prepare yourself for that," Dr. Grundy told him. "You both have long known that your daughter has very frail health.

It could not be expected that one with her constitution should live to any ripe age."

Margaret said, "But she will get better this time?"

"I hope so," the little doctor said with a sigh. "It will be touch and go. And she must be given careful attention if she does. No overdoing her strength. No excitement! She must be protected from shocks of any kind."

"We will look after all that," Jonas promised emotionally, "just so long as she lives."

"There will be careful nursing needed," the doctor went on. "I have a good woman in the village who is familiar with such cases. I will bring her out here until your daughter recovers."

"Spare no expense, Doctor," Jonas told him.

Dr. Grundy eyed him bleakly. "I'm afraid that money will not buy your daughter's life," he said. "But we will do all we can."

Greta's illness cast a fresh shadow over Collinwood. Margaret alternated with the nurse in the care of her desperately ill daughter. It was significant that when Greta regained consciousness the first person she asked to see was Barnabas.

He arrived promptly at dusk that evening, his gaunt face stricken with grief. As she met him in the hallway it came to her with a shock that he wore the same expression of sadness she'd noticed on the face in the portrait the day of Greta's attack. She promptly dismissed this as imagination.

Barnabas clasped her hand with his icy fingers. His voice was taut as he said, "I have come to do what I can." She disengaged her hand from his cold grip as soon as she could. "Greta has been asking for you."

"May I see her?"

"Only for a moment. And you must not excite her. The doctor has warned us that any strain could be fatal."

His gaunt, handsome face showed grief. "Your daughter is very precious to me," he said. "I had not realized how precious until now."

Margaret turned away. She did not want him to see that even in this moment of mutual sorrow she was unsure of her feelings about him. The repulsion she so often felt was frequently balanced by a sense of compassion. Had Barnabas not been doomed by that long-ago curse, she was sure he would have been a fine man. But as things were he was a divided soul—and she feared and distrusted the black side of his nature.

She said, "I'll take you in to her."

When Barnabas entered the shadowed sick room, Greta showed her first smile as she uttered his name weakly. And when Barnabas bent over her bed to touch his lips to her forehead it seemed the beginning of her recovery took place.

He was at her bedside all the evenings that followed. Even Jonas was impressed by his devotion. He confided in Margaret, "I have always considered Cousin Barnabas to be more than a little mad. But he has proven his worth at last."

Clare Blandish was one of those who also made regular visits to Collinwood during the most serious period of Greta's illness. She took Judith home with her to remain there until the crisis had passed and Margaret was able to give the girl regular attention.

On an afternoon some weeks after Greta's attack Margaret sat having tea with the attractive widow in the living room. She said, "I hope Judith isn't too much of a problem to you."

Clare smiled. "Of course she isn't. As a matter of fact, she's been extremely helpful. She has a knack for handling the younger children."

Margaret sighed. "Dr. Grundy says Greta should be fully recovered in a week or two. Of course she'll not be strong again, but I intend to keep the nurse on so I'll be able to devote my usual time to Judith after that."

Clare looked sympathetic. "I'm sure Judith is lonely and will be glad to return. Barnabas gives her some attention when he comes to visit and that helps."

"He is very devoted to her," Margaret said quietly.

The widow nodded. "Yes. But his devotion is of a strange nature. He seems most impressed because she resembles that portrait in your living room. He calls her his little Josette!" Clare shrugged over her teacup. "He is an odd man. I still do not understand him."

"But you are close friends," Margaret said meaningfully. Clare had taken to wearing high collars all the time which Margaret could only surmise hid the marks of the kisses Barnabas bestowed on her throat.

Clare's face clouded. "I am devoted to Barnabas," she said. "I will say no more than that."

Margaret looked down as she said, "I'm very troubled for Greta. Her happiness and now her very health seem to hinge on the presence of Barnabas. I shudder to think what might happen if he should decide to leave Collinsport."

"I can well understand your concern," Clare said quietly. "But I'm sure he will remain here."

Margaret said nothing to Clare of her other fears. It was not a subject she could discuss with anyone. Yet she lived in constant torment that Barnabas would make some violent move and upset the delicate balance of things. Patience continued to look sick, but she'd not been able to arrange for the maid to leave because of

Greta's unexpected illness. It was one of the first things she planned to do as soon as her daughter had recovered.

Several times when the nurse was taking care of Greta she went out in the early evening in the hope of meeting Barnabas and having a private talk with him about Patience. She felt she might persuade him to leave the girl alone now that she was able to fight off his hypnotic spell. But whenever she knocked at the door of the old house there was no answer.

She guessed that Barnabas had given Hare orders not to answer the door. She went around to the cellar entrance which she had used and saw a new padlock on it. Unless she found some other way to get into the house she might never be able to confront Barnabas alone.

After one visit to the old house she went on beyond it. Crossing the wide field, she continued until she reached the small cemetery. She had not been there since the day of Granny Entwhistle's funeral. All that seemed so long ago now. She slowly made her way between the weatherbeaten stones marking the neat mounds until she came to the giant vault that housed the caskets of the original members of the Collins family. She was astonished to see that the iron door to the tomb was a few inches open.

Moving closer, she grasped the handle of the rusty door and tried to move it. It creaked open slowly when she exerted her full strength. And now she could look inside. She saw there were several stone steps descending to a floor perhaps two feet below the ground surface. On each wall of the tomb there were shelves with coffins on them. She could not see clearly enough to take in much detail except to know that it was dusty and gray. This was the tomb which Hare had visited and robbed.

She decided to take a step inside to see if the coffins visible to her showed any sign of having been broken into. She had an idea there were others far in the shadows at the rear of the tomb and it might have been these that Hare had so callously vandalized.

The stench of the grave assailed her nostrils as she nervously took another step down into the interior of the old vault. And she began to tremble slightly. Here she was surrounded by the remains of those whose portraits graced the walls of Collinwood. Was the lovely Josette in one of those mildewed caskets, a sorry heap of dust and bones with maybe a precious trinket or two amid the decay to identify her remains? She frowned at the thought. She had read the name Josette on that worn red marble stone, but there could have been more than one of that name.

She stood there uncertainly, lost in her thoughts. And then without any warning the iron door of the tomb was slammed closed behind her. She screamed as she found herself in darkness. Turning, she beat her hands frantically against the rusty door.

"Let me out! Please! You've locked me in here!" she cried in terror.

But her words echoed hollowly in the blackness of the tomb and no one made any reply. Great sobs filled her throat as she turned and peered into the dark depths of the vault. Turning back, she beat on the ancient iron again until her knuckles were skinned and bleeding.

It could have been no accident. Nor had a gust of wind closed the door. It would take the application of superior strength. Hare's malicious ape-face crossed her mind. Undoubtedly he had covertly followed her to the cemetery and waited for his chance to play this macabre trick on her.

Half-mad with fear, she resumed what surely must be a futile assault on the door. She had barely begun when to her shocked relief the rusty door creaked open again. Silhouetted against the fading light outside were the head and shoulders of the retarded Luke Sinnot. The young man was crouching down so he could peer into the tomb.

Margaret quickly stepped outside and gave the youth an angry look. "Did you close that door, Luke?"

He shook his head. "No. It was Hare!"

"Are you certain?"

"I was down by the trees watching when you came to the cemetery and he was only a little way behind you, ma'am."

She only half-believed him. "Why didn't you warn me?"

The blank-faced young man said, "I was afraid. I knew Hare would fix me if he saw me."

"Do you often spy on him this way?"

"I come down here and wait," Luke said slyly. "Some nights it is Hare who comes and other nights it's the tall one."

"Cousin Barnabas?"

"Yes."

"I don't think you should come down here as you've been doing," she told him. "I mean that for your own good. Still, I'm thankful you were here tonight or I might still be in there." She looked down at her bleeding knuckles and the fingernails broken in her frantic effort to escape. She felt weary and shaken.

"I watched him close the door," Luke said gleefully. "And then I waited for him to leave before I came to let you out."

"I would have felt a lot easier if I'd known you were out there ready to rescue me," she told him ruefully.

She allowed Luke to escort her back to the house, convinced now that Hare had deliberately tried to get rid of her by locking her in the lonely tomb. He had counted on no one visiting the isolated family cemetery to rescue her, not knowing that Luke was watching him from the shelter of the neighboring evergreens. Had Hare done this on his own, or had he been acting on the orders of Barnabas?

The following morning Ada came to her as soon as she appeared downstairs. The little maid was in a dreadful state. "Patience went out last night and didn't come back," she told Margaret. "I heard a scream after she left and I know something dreadful has happened to her!"

Icy fear gripped Margaret. She sensed that this was the crisis she had been praying would never come. "Have you searched the grounds?"

"Luke has looked around," Ada said on the verge of tears. "There isn't a sign of her anywhere. I know that devil has done away with her!" And the maid lifted her apron ends to dab at her eyes.

The reference to Barnabas alarmed Margaret more. She said, "You mustn't lose control of yourself! And whatever happens, Miss Greta mustn't know about this. She is in no fit state for such news."

"Yes, ma'am," Ada said. "But we have to try and find her. Though I don't expect it will be alive!"

She patted the girl's arm. "You mustn't take the worst view. It may turn out well yet. She may come back on her own."

Jonas was now descending the stairs. He stared at her and the girl. "What is the trouble here?"

Margaret quickly told him and suggested, "I think a proper search should be made for her!"

Jonas stood there with his hand on the bannister frowning. "The young hussy has probably run off with some man. Why should we concern ourselves?"

"It's more than that, sir," Ada said, forgetting her lowly station in her agitation. "I think your cousin in the old house has done away with her!"

Margaret gave her a warning look to keep silent and the girl at once stepped back with a frightened expression. Jonas came on down the stairs and confronted Margaret. "What does this girl mean by speaking about Cousin Barnabas in that fashion?"

"She's overwrought. It's been a strain on her," Margaret apologized for the girl.

"Overwrought, indeed!" Jonas said with sarcasm. "I should think she is." And glaring at the girl, he snapped, "See that you make no more such ridiculous accusations!"

Margaret said, "Greta mustn't be disturbed by this."

"No reason why she should be," Jonas said. "We can warn the other servants not to mention it to her. I'd say this is a task for the town constable."

Jerry Lee, the Collinsport constable, drove up in a buggy

during the noon hour. Jonas had left for the factory, so the constable introduced himself to Margaret. He was a stout man with a solemn face, heavy-lidded eyes and a slow way of moving and talking.

"I reckon we'll have to search the house and grounds thorough, ma'am."

"Just so long as you don't bother my daughter, Greta," she told the police officer. "She is confined to her room, recovering from a severe heart attack."

He doffed his battered felt hat and scratched his graying hair. "I guess we can skip her room as long as I have your word the girl ain't hiding in there."

"She's not in there. I can promise you that," Margaret declared.

She waited silently while the constable and his helpers searched the grounds and house, knowing that sooner or later the name of Barnabas would come up. And she didn't know what she would say. If he had hurt Patience she felt she could no longer protect him. The police could put him safely away as they would any other criminally mad man. But could they keep him behind bars? She doubted it.

She went in to visit Greta and found her invalid daughter sitting propped up in bed with several pillows behind her.

Greta gave her a troubled look. "What is going on this morning? There is a tenseness about everyone. What is it?"

She forced a smile. "It is nothing. Just your imagination. You must be feeling better to allow your nerves to get so on edge."

"I'm not a child, Mother," Greta protested. "If something has happened, tell me!"

"I have told you," Margaret said. "You're making a lot over nothing. Now try and relax." And she left the room before Greta had a chance to question her more.

She had barely reached the living room when Constable Lee came to see her again. "We've gone over the main house and outbuildings and searched the grounds with a fine-tooth comb," he said. "She isn't anywhere!"

"Then she may have ran off," Margaret said hopefully.

The constable looked skeptical. "Her sister doesn't seem to think so," he informed her. "And now I've come to ask you about the old house. I should take a look in there but I can't get anyone to answer the door."

"My husband's cousin, Barnabas, has been living there," she said in a small voice. "He and his servant may have gone off on holiday for the day."

Constable Lee eyed her suspiciously. "You got no keys to the place?"

"Not any longer," she said, trying to hide her fear. "Cousin Barnabas is a recluse. He insists on his privacy."

The Constable frowned. "That the one who drops in at the Blue Whale some nights, a tall feller with a kind of strange way? Wears a coat with a cape over it?"

"Yes."

"I've seen him. Keeps to himself always. Can you people vouch for him?"

"He's a quiet, retiring man," Margaret said. "I doubt if he'd be able to help you even if he were here."

The constable considered. "I'll still have to take a look in that house before I leave," he said. "You got any suggestions how I might get in?"

She hesitated. "There is a cellar door. I once used it. But it has a new padlock. The wood is old and rotted. I don't think you'd have too much trouble prying it open."

"Would you mind coming along and showing me?"

"No," she said quietly. "Not if you'd like me to. It's really fairly easy to find. It's at the rear of the house."

"I'd rather you was there," Constable Lee said. "Makes it a bit more legal since I have to force entry."

She accompanied him and the other two men, knowing full well they would not find Barnabas. He would be in the secret room. And under the circumstances she doubted if Hare would be there either. He would have run off somewhere to hide. She was going to have to make some important decisions shortly. She was convinced Patience had been murdered and in all probability by Barnabas. The question was, would she now tell what she knew about him? And if she did, would anyone believe her?

But the main thing forcing her to keep silent was the worry of what this might do to Greta. It would be a dreadful shock to her if Barnabas was taken into custody as a killer. And any sudden shock could result in her death.

They came to the brooding old house and she showed them where the cellar door was. It took the constable only a minute to slide a crowbar under the lock and splinter the fittings away from the rotted wood. He surveyed his work grimly and lifted the door open. "Now we'll take a look in there," he announced.

She waited until they had made their way upstairs and opened the front door for her from the inside. She was sick with apprehension as the constable led her from room to room in the grim old mansion.

He had a disgusted look on his fat, florid face. "Except for the living room and that little room in the back the servant used, this place seems as if there'd been no one in it. Your Cousin

Barnabas hasn't even taken the covers off the furniture in most of the rooms."

"He's a very strange man," she agreed.

"And he certainly ain't around here, or that Hare either," Constable Lee said with some exasperation. "I figure he knows exactly what happened to that pretty little Patience."

She gave him a troubled glance. "Why do you say that?"

"He's the logical suspect and he's run away. His servant too!"

"Do you think the girl is with them?" she asked.

The constable frowned again. "Maybe and then again, maybe not. I got to go slow on this one."

They had finished their search of the house and were leaving by the front door when a man came running across the open field, waving his arms wildly to attract their attention. Margaret felt another surge of fear. He was coining from the direction of the cemetery.

Constable Lee at once looked happier. "That's my other man," he said. "I sent him out to check the field. Reckon he's turned up something." And he strode out across the grass to meet the running man.

Margaret hurried after him and was at his side when the man came breathlessly to a halt in front of them. One look at his terrified face told her everything.

He gasped, "I found the girl! She's dead. Somebody strangled her."

CHAPTER 10

"Where did you find her?" the constable asked.

"By the Collins tomb," his helper said, still breathing with difficulty. "Somebody had opened the door of the tomb and was getting ready to hide the body in there when I came along."

Margaret had a difficult time stifling a cry of terror. She recalled the tomb all too vividly. And she had no doubt it had been Hare who'd dragged the body to the cemetery to dispose of it there while Barnabas remained safely in that hidden room.

Lee looked pleased. "Got any idea who it was?"

"No. I just caught a glimpse of his coat tails," the man said. "But he made a run of it for the woods. He must still be hiding out there."

"We'll get all the men together and take a look," Lee said. Then he turned to Margaret. "Well, at least we know what happened to the girl now. And as soon as we latch onto that fellow in the woods, we'll have the answer to who strangled her."

She was on the verge of telling him he was wrong and leading him to the secret room and Barnabas. But she couldn't do that, not without placing her daughter's life in jeopardy. And she dare not risk it! Better to let them arrest Hare if they could find him. She doubted that they would.

"We should be back pretty soon," the constable told her.

She noticed for the first time he was carrying a gun. She wondered vaguely if the others were armed and guessed they were. They left in a body, the groom joining them, and fanned out as they reached the field.

She watched them go and when they were a safe distance off she turned and quickly made her way down the cellar steps. She was trembling as she groped her way along the length of the dank underground area. At last she reached the wall which contained the secret entrance to the hidden room and explored it with anxious fingers until she found the strip of molding which controlled it.

The panel swung in to reveal the ghostly, gray room. Candles still flickered on the sideboard. The coffin was in its usual place with the lid closed. Margaret approached it with a pounding heart.

When she was close to it she reached out to raise the lid. It took a supreme effort on her part to find the courage to make this move. Very slowly she lifted it to expose the sleeping Barnabas. His expression was grim as if he were the victim of some dreadful nightmare, which seemed quite likely in view of the circumstances. The eyes beneath the shaggy black brows were tightly closed and his raven-black hair was pressed against the flesh-colored satin of the casket's pillow. His hands were folded and the strange black ring stood out against their pasty dead appearance. They were the hands of a corpse!

But what riveted her horrified attention was the tiny trickle of bright red blood which dribbled from the right corner of his mouth. The blood of poor dead Patience whom he'd kissed for a final time before throttling her? She was revolted and yet she could not turn away from the placid figure in the coffin.

Why had he found it necessary to murder Patience? Had the quarrel between them become so serious? She blamed herself for not acting sooner. She had known and been warned. Now it was too late. They were all involved. And the revelation that Barnabas was a cold-blooded killer could certainly prove fatal for her invalid daughter.

Knowing she had not been able to think it out enough yet, she carefully lowered the coffin lid. She would let Barnabas continued his tormented sleep until dusk came to release him. Time enough to confront him with his crime then.

With a final glance at the closed casket she quickly left the cold gray room and sealed it again. Making sure the panel concealing the room's entrance was properly in place, she groped her way along the earthen floor to the stairs leading to the open. When she stepped up onto the grass she took a deep breath and tried to shut her mind to the horror she had just seen.

She started to walk back to Collinwood at a deliberate pace and had only gone a short distance when she heard the shots from the cemetery. She halted with a look of fear shadowing her face. Had they caught up with Hare so quickly? Would he pay the debt for his master's crime? She felt a brief moment of sympathy for the ugly man.

Changing direction, she began walking toward the path that led to the cemetery. She had gone halfway across the broad field and could see the cemetery and the cluster of men standing near the woods beyond it. She kept on walking certain now they had either shot or captured Hare. As she drew near the cemetery she saw the constable leave his men and come forward to meet her.

He joined her just inside the cemetery gate. "We got him," he said. "Spotted him in the woods and gave him a warning. But he kept on running."

"Did you shoot him?" she asked, a tremor in her voice.

The old constable looked grim. "Had to! He wouldn't halt when we ordered him to. No wonder, after what he'd done."

Margaret swallowed hard. "Are you sure it was him?"

"Had to be," Constable Lee said. "Skulking there watching us,"

"Is he dead?"

"Yep," he sighed. "Reckon I got him with my first bullet. Probably better this way. Saves the fuss and expense of a trial."

"As long as you're sure it was Hare," she said in a small voice. The temptation to speak out again was strong, to tell the over-confident lawman that he had made a ghastly mistake—that the murderer of Patience was sleeping in a coffin in the cellar of the old house. But would he listen to her? Would he believe her even if she took him to where Barnabas was? Wouldn't he think Barnabas was merely a crazy man with a servant who had committed a brutal murder? She would have threatened Greta's life for nothing! Better to remain quiet.

"What's that about Hare?" Constable Lee asked with an odd look.

"As long as you're sure it was the servant," she said.

Lee raised his eyebrows. "You got it all wrong," he told her. "It wasn't the deaf and dumb one. It was Luke Sinnot!"

It was then she fainted. When she came to minutes later the constable was bending over her worriedly. "Sorry to shock you like that, Mrs. Collins," he apologized. "I should have known better."

"It's all right," she said weakly, making an effort to sit up.

He helped her to her feet. "Sure you're able to stand?"

"Yes," she said, avoiding his anxious eyes. "I'll be perfectly all right. It was stupid of me to faint."

"I should have guessed how you'd feel about that boy," the Constable went on sympathetically. "You brought him here and gave him a good job. Course he weren't never right in the head. I always thought you were taking a big risk."

"Please. I'd rather not talk about it," she said, almost on the point of collapse again. That it should have been poor innocent Luke who'd had to take on the burden of the crime!

"You're lucky, Mrs. Collins," the constable said. "Look at it that way. Luke used to wheel your girl around. He could have strangled her instead of Patience."

Mention of Greta brought to mind the seriousness of her dilemma. She turned to the constable quickly. "Because of the precarious state of my daughter's health, I do not want her to find out about all this."

"Sure. I understand."

"I'll tell her that Patience and Luke have left to take better jobs somewhere else," she went on.

"Me and the boys will take the bodies into the village," Constable Lee promised her. "We'll keep everything quiet around here. And I hope your girl will be all right."

"Thank you, Constable," she said sincerely. "It seems nothing else has equal importance for me these days."

And then she started back to Collinwood alone. Her legs were weak under her so that she stumbled several times as she crossed the wide uneven field. Nauseated, she knew she would never be able to erase the shame and horror from her conscience. It would be another dread thing to live with, as she had lived with Granny Entwhistle's murder!

But Greta had to be protected. Her lovely and frail daughter might still live a few years if nothing disturbed her placid routine. And no matter what torment it brought her, Margaret was bound to keep silent for her only child's sake. She would never dare share her burden with Jonas. The only person on earth with whom she could whisper of this was Barnabas Collins! The murderer!

Margaret avoided going to Greta's room until she had regained some confidence. And when she told the girl that both Patience and Luke had left service at Collinwood to go seek employment elsewhere, Greta's reaction was one of hurt dismay.

"Luke went away without even saying goodbye?" she said unhappily.

"A wagon came for them," Margaret said in a lie that was close to the truth. "Luke had very little time."

"But it's not like him!" Greta mourned.

Margaret looked down at her. "You mustn't feel so badly about it," she said placatingly.

"But I've been counting the days until he would be wheeling me out on the lawn again! Now he never will. Perhaps I shall never see the lawn again, either!"

"What ridiculous talk!" Margaret scoffed. "I'll wheel you out there myself. And Judith will be back. She's growing up. She'll be happy to go with you!"

Greta turned her head away despondently, her frail lovely face shadowed with sorrow. "There is only Cousin Barnabas left to me now," she said. "Dear Cousin Barnabas."

Margaret stiffened at the mention of his name. Then she forced herself to say evenly, "Yes. You will still have Cousin Barnabas."

When Jonas returned from the plant that evening he was thoroughly upset. Margaret had been prepared for this, knowing him so well. She at once handed him his first before-dinner glass of sherry.

He took it, staring at her. "How can you be so calm after what happened here today?"

"I have no choice," she said. "There is Greta to consider." She told him the story she had given Greta, and that she'd warned the servants to stick to the same version of events. "So you must collect yourself, as well."

Jonas gulped down his sherry and handed her the glass to be refilled. His gray side-whiskers seemed to bristle on his florid face. The irreverent thought struck her that he had come by the side-whiskers too late; they were old-fashioned, now. Fortune, too, had come to Jonas in laggard fashion and found him without the ability to properly enjoy it.

She handed him another sherry. "When you enter Greta's room you must take none of this upset with you," she warned.

He nodded impatiently. "Don't you think I'm intelligent enough to realize that?"

"Your intentions are good," she said. "But you are far too easy to read. And Greta is quick to catch a mood."

Jonas frowned as he sipped the second sherry and calmed a trifle. "What about Barnabas?" he asked. "I suppose my mad cousin didn't budge from the house. His everlasting experiments are all that are important to him, although he never seems to achieve any ends with them!"

She looked down. "I did not see him outside."

"I saw that servant of his skulking into the old house as I drove by in my carriage," Jonas said darkly. "I don't like the fellow! In fact, I don't much care for my precious cousin either. If it weren't that Greta is so devoted to him I'd send that lot packing! I don't need the rental anymore."

"No, you don't," she said. But that had come too late—like everything else, she thought. Now Barnabas was a fact of their lives.

Her husband finished his sherry. "I suppose I'd better go

speak to Greta before dinner."

She nodded. "Remember!"

She followed him into the sickroom a few minutes later, wanting to be sure he made no errors and also to get him out of the room as soon as she conveniently could. He was putting on a very neat show of casual good humor. Greta seemed relaxed and unaware of the dark happenings of the day. Then she suddenly created an awkward moment by asking an unexpected question.

"I heard gunshots this morning," she said innocently. "Do you know what they were about?"

Jonas turned a deep scarlet and with a pleading glance at Margaret, murmured, "I was at the office all morning."

"A farmer's boy out after some rabbits," Margaret spoke up at once. "I often hear them in the woods."

"I wish they wouldn't hunt so near the house," Greta said with a tiny shudder. "I hate to think of those poor little creatures being murdered."

Jonas looked apoplectic once again and cleared his throat. "Now, now," he said. "We mustn't be too sensitive about such things."

Margaret stepped forward and smiled at her daughter. "I'm sure we've stayed too long. You're tired and I know your father is hungry."

Greta looked up from her pillow wistfully. "Please send Cousin Barnabas in as soon as he oomes. I feel so lonely."

"You can be sure I will," Margaret promised as she led her husband to the door.

When they were outside and a safe distance from the room he removed a handkerchief from his upper pocket and mopped his brow with it. "That was close," he said. "I was grateful for your being there."

"I felt you might need me," she said coolly. She was surprising herself with the calm that she'd achieved—especially since beneath her cool exterior she was writhing from the torments of her conscience. But the need to save her daughter had made this abnormal assurance possible. She only hoped she would be able to maintain it.

By exerting the same control she managed to get Jonas into his study and at work before dusk arrived—and Barnabas. She wanted her husband safely out of the way when she had this meeting with his cousin. While she did not know exactly what she was going to say to Barnabas, it would be nothing for her husband's ears.

As it turned out, she was in Greta's room when he arrived. Ada came into the room, still looking pale and drawn, and told her, "Mr. Barnabas has arrived, ma'am."

"Tell him I'll be right out."

Greta raised herself anxiously from the pillow. "Why not have him come in here?"

"Because I'd like to greet him first," Margaret said calmly. "You really mustn't be so possessive of Cousin Barnabas. And in any case it will give you a few minutes to have your nurse beautify you for him."

Leaving Greta placated she went on out to meet Barnabas Collins. He was in the living room, standing before the portrait of Josette and studying it seriously in the mellow glow from the single lamp of the crystal chandelier, so absorbed he apparently wasn't aware of her entrance.

When she had come to stand beside him she joined him in staring at the oil portrait which so much resembled her own daughter and also the girl Judith. In a quiet voice, she said, "Patience wore Josette's dress and played her part night after night for you. Why did you kill her?"

Barnabas turned his gaze to her, looking somewhat startled. "Why do you say that?"

"Because I am certain that you murdered the poor girl."

The handsome, gaunt face showed uneasiness. "I understand that your handyman Luke Sinnot was responsible. At least that is what the police believe. Why should you think differently?"

"Because I know all the facts about you and Patience," she said evenly.

"You are becoming tiresome," he told her with a touch of arrogance. "I would not come here if it were not for Greta's sake. I would take Judith and leave Collinsport."

"Not while Greta needs you."

"I don't take orders from you."

"You will in the future," she told him with a grim note of warning in her voice. "The only reason I have spared you in this wretched business is because of Greta."

Barnabas stood there in his caped coat staring at her with tormented eyes. His fingers restlessly clenched and unclenched the silver wolf's head of his cane. "You do not understand," he told her in a low tense voice. "You do not try to understand. Have you any idea what my life is like? How long I have endured Angelique's curse? How I pray to one day be restored to a normal existence?"

She eyed him reproachfully. "I only know you have killed again. And I would not keep silent except for Greta."

"Patience had come to know me for the unhappy creature that I am," he went on quickly. "I no longer could induce her to forget. Her love for me turned to hatred when I would not meet her impossible demands."

"What impossible demands?"

"That I marry her," Barnabas said. "And you know such a thing was out of the question. I'm dedicating my life to young Judith. One day she will be the living image of that portrait. And our marriage will void the curse and I shall become a whole man again!"

"An insane dream!" Margaret told him scornfully. "It will never come to pass."

He lifted his cane as if to strike her, his face contorted with a sudden anger. Then apparently he lowered the cane again and stared at her sullenly. "I will not listen to you," he said. "I will not believe you."

She shrugged. "Delude yourself if you like. Greta is waiting for you. And remember, she knows nothing of the murder or Luke's being shot. She thinks both Patience and Luke have gone to other employment. Say nothing to upset her belief."

Barnabas studied her solemnly. "I'm doing this for Greta's sake," he said. "You couldn't force me to it. There is no direct evidence to connect me with the murder."

"Evidence enough, I think," she said. "But we needn't discuss it since we understand each other so well. Greta is waiting."

He stared at her a moment longer as if he were going to reply. Then he seemed to change his mind and strode past her to the hallway and Greta's room.

Only then did the reaction take hold of her. She weakly sank into a nearby chair, trembling as if stricken with ague. Barnabas Collins was a madman and a murderer. And she had made herself his accomplice. Could she ever expect to be forgiven?

In the months that followed the murder became less a topic of conversation. No one questioned that Luke Sinnot had committed the crime. There was no family to argue indignantly on the retarded young man's behalf. Margaret, who could have pleaded his innocence, did not.

Judith had returned to Collinwood and Margaret took great pleasure in directing her studies. The girl was alert and would one day be a credit to her. Greta now enjoyed a measure of health and was able to move about the house in her wheelchair as before. But she still looked ill and the doctor continued to warn against exposing her to any strain.

Barnabas Collins had gradually cut his visits to the house to three times a week, avoiding Margaret whenever he could and acting in a guilty manner when they met. But he continued to be his charming self where Greta was concerned and that was all she asked. She understood he was spending a great deal of his time with the attractive widow, Clare Blandish. But she could not be sure of this since Clare had unaccountably stopped visiting her.

In December Margaret had the groom take her to the village in the sleigh to do some Christmas shopping in the general store. A light snowstorm had left a good layer of snow on the road for easy sledding and had mantled the evergreens in white beauty. When she had finished at the general store she had the groom stop by Clare's big yellow and white mansion.

Clare answered the door herself and Margaret was shocked to note how pale and emaciated the pretty widow had become. And she found it even stranger that Clare apparently was not glad to see her.

Gathering a dark shawl around her shoulders, Clare said, "I wasn't expecting visitors."

Margaret forced a smile. "Come now! There is nothing formal about one old friend calling on another. I have only a few minutes to stay. But I did want to see you before the holidays."

"I have not been well," Clare said, stepping back with some reluctance to let her enter.

Margaret stared at her as she closed the door. "You do look ill! And I've worried that I've not heard from you. Judith has missed you as well."

Clare joined her, the pinched face shadowed. "My plans have been upset," she said in a dull voice. "Because of the way things have been I've had to give up with the children. I sent them to an orphanage in Portland. And I have given the institution a sum of money for their care."

"But that is not like you!" she protested. "The children were your life." And her eyes fixed on Clare's throat and she saw the widow was still wearing a high collar. So she asked, "Are you seeing Barnabas?"

Clare looked startled. She made the gesture of pulling the shawl protectively about her again. "Yes, I see him," she said. "But it is no longer the same friendship."

"Oh?" Margaret was not only distressed by her friend's abject frame of mind but she was also beginning to detect a familiar note in her behavior. She was acting as Patience had before she was murdered.

Clare gave her a plaintive look. "In the beginning knowing Barnabas was like a beautiful dream. Now the beautiful dream has become a nightmare. I see things about him I didn't before." She paused, her eyes filled with terror. "Can you guess the kind of person he is?"

"I think so," she said quietly.

"You can't!" Clare protested. "Or you wouldn't stand there so calmly."

Margaret had no idea how much her friend had discovered

about Barnabas. And she didn't care to inquire. To reveal what she herself knew would be to threaten Greta's life.

"I'll offer you some advice," she told the distraught widow. "I think you should get away from here and Barnabas as soon as possible."

"But I love him!" Clare wailed. "I would like to marry him!"

She shook her head. "Hopeless! He'll never marry you."

"I know," her friend said, looking away. "He told me so bluntly after imposing on my friendship all this time. He can be cruel!"

"I'm only too aware of that."

"And yet he has another side. There are times when he can be wonderful. So much charm! So considerate! But you never know when he'll change. And lately it has been his dark side I've seen mostly."

Margaret put an arm around her friend. "Promise me you'll think seriously about going away for a while. Anywhere that you can be free of Barnabas."

"Perhaps after the New Year," Clare said.

"Don't wait!" Margaret pleaded. Then she said goodbye and went out to the waiting sleigh. All during the drive back to Collinwood she worried about Clare. And for long after that.

She sought out a few minutes with Barnabas Collins alone during one of his visits to the house. "What are you doing to Clare?" she demanded.

He shrugged. "Nothing."

"She claims you have made her desperately unhappy."

The gaunt, handsome face took on an expression of ironic amusement. "I cannot help it if she gets the idea I am madly in love with her and willing to make her my wife."

"You have used her!" Margaret reminded him firmly. "If she has that notion you are to blame."

"I might have expected you to take sides against me," he said with a sigh. "I only continue seeing her out of pity."

Margaret gave him a meaningful look. "From what she said she knows your secret. And if you incur her hatred she may tell it to others. You should be mindful of that."

The man in the Inverness cape looked less happy as he hesitated in the foyer before leaving. "You misjudge her," he said. "She will say nothing."

Margaret hoped her warning might do some good, that Barnabas would take a hint and stop seeing Clare Blandish. It might hurt the widow for a time but it would be better for her in the long run. Now that she was disillusioned with Barnabas it would be best for her to forget him.

The holidays came and went. January was a month of bitter weather and Collinwood became an island in a sea of snow. From her window Margaret occasionally saw a wisp of smoke rise from one of the chimneys of the old house. She surmised it was the surly Hare trying to keep himself from freezing. She shivered involuntarily as she thought of Barnabas down in that icy room in his coffin. He required no fire to keep him warm.

And when he paid his visits to Greta he wore exactly the same Inverness cape as he had on the hottest nights of summer. Nor did he don a hat. He would enter from a stormy night with his hair glistening with snow and seem to be unaware of it. But then wasn't he really a sort of ghost? And what did ghosts care about the weather?

CHAPTER 11

Occupied with the daily problems at Collinwood during this terrible winter, Margaret put Clare Blandish out of her mind for a while. But this was changed one below-zero night in late January when there was a loud knocking on the front door just as she was about ready to go upstairs to bed.

She opened the door and stood back to gain a little protection from the biting cold. A muffled, apologetic figure whom she recognized as Clare Blandish's coachman bowed from the snow-covered front step. "I've come for Mrs. Blandish," the coachmen said in a husky voice.

Margaret was startled. "I'm sorry. She isn't here."

The man's red face, which barely showed above his woolen scarf, registered amazement. "But I brought her here early tonight. And she told me to come back for her."

"You must be mistaken."

"No, ma'am," the groom said in distress, "she left the sleigh right at this door."

She tried to collect her thoughts. There could no longer be any question that the man on the doorstep was telling the truth. So what had happened to Clare? Why hadn't she come on into the house as she'd planned? The only explanation she could think of was that the pretty widow had never intended to visit her. She had gone on to the old mansion to see Barnabas Collins!

The picture of that bleak old house on this below-zero night was not a comforting one. Clare would freeze there. She would not be aware of the eerie fact that Barnabas was impervious to the cold. And Barnabas could well be out on one of his after-dark prowls. In which case Clare could have been greeted by the frightening Hare. Margaret was terrified of what might have happened.

The attractive widow had now been missing for several hours. She had to be either at the old house or somewhere out in the cold.

"Come inside for a moment," she invited the groom.

"Thanks, ma'am," the old man replied anxiously. "I'm fair worried."

She closed the door behind him. "You may well be." She hurried upstairs to notify Jonas.

The result was that Jonas, along with two of the stable men and Clare's groom set out for the old house in search of the missing woman. Margaret rushed to the kitchen and peered out the almost completely frosted window to catch a final glimpse of the small band as they went past the bam. The two lanterns carried by them sparkled in the cold night. She watched until they were out of sight.

The little maid, Ada, stood anxiously at her shoulder. "What do you think has happened to her, ma'am?"

Margaret turned to gaze at the frightened girl's pale face. "I haven't any idea," she said. "I'm puzzled she didn't come directly in here as she'd evidently intended."

Ada looked solemn. "I know why."

"You do?"

"He got her! You couldn't pay me to go out there after dark! Not after all that has happened!"

"Who do you mean?" Margaret asked sharply, knowing what the answer would be.

"Him! Barnabas! Who else?" Ada demanded. "He killed Patience and now it's Mrs. Blandish's turn. Granny Entwhistle was right when she said he had brought a curse to Collinwood!"

"You mustn't let an old woman's wanderings influence you," she warned the girl, afraid Ada might denounce Barnabas to others. Then the whole house of cards would collapse and Greta would learn the truth about the man she idolized—a truth that would kill her.

Ada looked sullen. "Is there anything you want me to do, ma'am?"

She nodded. It would be wise to keep the girl occupied. "I think you should prepare a warm beverage for the men when they return." And she went back to her post at the frosted window to try and catch sight of them when they reappeared. As she peered out into the starry, winter night a wolf howled weirdly from a far distance and caused her to shudder.

It was perhaps thirty minutes later when she first caught a glimpse of the lanterns swinging and saw the small group returning. She gasped and raised a hand to her mouth as she noted they were carrying something. It almost surely had to be the missing Clare!

Jonas was the first to enter the kitchen. He stood in the doorway a moment stamping the snow from his shoes. Then he advanced to her with a grave expression. "We found her. She's dead."

"Oh, no!" Margaret was wide-eyed with shock and distress.

He nodded. "The men are putting her body in the sleigh now."

"Where was she?"

Jonas frowned. "I don't understand it. Her tracks led to the old house. Then they went from the front steps of the house toward the cemetery. We found her stretched out on the ground a short distance from the Collins tomb. She'd fallen and died from exposure. Now what would take her out there on a night like this?"

Margaret bit her lip as she fought for control. Tears blurred her eyes. She shook her head. "I can't imagine. Did you talk to anyone at the old house? Barnabas or his servant?"

"No one answered the door," her husband said. "And the entire house appeared to be in darkness. There's something strange about those two. I wish we'd never had them on the place!"

"But you did," she said quietly. "Were there any other foot tracks in the snow in addition to Clare's?"

"None," Jonas said. "That's the puzzling part of it. What made her stray out there alone?"

Margaret glanced from her husband to the maid who was standing by the stove with a stricken look on her young face. Very quietly she said, "She must have been confused after she visited the old house and found Barnabas gone. She wandered out there instead of returning here."

Jonas looked dubious. "Doesn't seem to make sense," he said. "The men will be coming in for something to warm them. Better get it ready."

In the end Margaret's supposition that Clare Blandish had become confused in the cold and darkness and taken the wrong direction was accepted. It was agreed she'd been unstable for some months and many whispered that she had finally lost her mind completely. Margaret mildly encouraged this opinion since it offered the most logical explanation for the lovely widow's death.

She was, however, sure Barnabas Collins had contributed to Clare's death in some fashion. But she couldn't be certain how. The fact there had been no footprints in the snow other than Clare's seemed to indicate he had not lured her to the graveyard or been there with her. And when Margaret queried him about her friend's death he pretended complete innocence, claiming he and Hare had gone into the village to visit the Blue Whale Tavern that night.

Yet she continued to wonder. And then one February evening she made a discovery that cleared up much of the mystery for her. It had snowed lightly and when she opened the front door to allow Barnabas to enter for one of his regular visits with Greta her eyes happened to wander to the step and the path leading to it. There were no footprints in the fresh snow!

So Barnabas left no revealing tracks behind him in the snow! She closed the door and faced the tall, gaunt man accusingly.

"So that's it," she said. "That's why they didn't find your footprints beside Clare's that night!"

The man in the Inverness cape gave her an ironic smile. "You are always coming up with the wildest theories concerning me."

"Don't deny it!" Margaret told him bitterly. "You were making one of your night visits to Josette's tomb. Clare saw you crossing the field toward the cemetery and followed you. And you let her die out there as she tried to locate you. Probably you hid in the shadows of the tomb and watched as she collapsed!"

"I find that fantastic!" Barnabas said haughtily.

Margaret sighed. "Be good to Greta," she said in a grim voice. "She is the one reason I'm not unmasking you for what you are!"

CHAPTER 12

And in spite of his macabre behavior Barnabas was a charming and gentle companion to her desperately ill daughter. Greta seldom managed to leave her bed in the months that followed. Even the warm days of the brief Maine summer brought no improvement in her condition. The months stretched into years, and as she grew more languid and her pallor became chronic her only pleasure seemed to be the hours spent in his company.

He would tell her of his travels in England and the Continent and with the magic of his personality take her far from the confines of her sickroom. While Margaret stood by and listened at these moments, she became almost ready to forgive the gaunt, handsome man for his other crimes. He was driven ruthlessly by that long-ago curse and forever seeking to free himself of it.

And he was convinced he could only do this through marriage with his Josette. Or with someone who closely resembled her. Greta once had, but with the fading caused by her illness the resemblance had almost vanished. On the other hand, as time went by, Judith was blossoming into full womanhood and increasingly looking more like the portrait in the living room.

Now a comely young woman of eighteen, Judith, under Margaret's tutelage, had grown into an intelligent and lovely girl.

She was devoted to Greta and seemingly unaware of the unnatural interest in her exhibited by her foster father, Barnabas. She accepted his attentions and presents happily as those of a devoted father. Not knowing what Margaret knew, the girl thought of him as a charming but eccentric older man.

Margaret, who now regarded Judith as her own, was aware that the moment was soon at hand when Barnabas would insist on claiming Judith as his bride. Daily he was becoming more restless. His interest in Greta was visibly less and he prevailed on Judith to join him whenever he visited the sick girl.

Over the years Margaret knew that Barnabas had been involved with several of the village girls of easy virtue. And when one of them had been discovered dead on the beach not far from the waterfront location of the Collins Shipping Company she had not been too surprised. Fortunately no one had linked Barnabas with the murder and the aging Dr. Grundy had apparently missed any unusual marks on the girl's neck. The doctor put the death down to misadventure by drowning.

From gossip that reached Collinwood by the servants Margaret also knew Barnabas was actively courting a barmaid at the Blue Whale Tavern. And it took her only a short time to discover the girl made a habit of wearing a high collar. This cleared up the question of where he was securing his regular supply of human blood now that Clare had been dead for several years.

For a time Margaret had hoped that Barnabas might tire of the restricted existence of Collinwood and leave. He had not changed any in physical appearance during his long stay in the old house while Hare, his servant, had become much more gray but no less surly. The increasing interest Barnabas was exhibiting in Judith killed any hopes Margaret clung to that he would wander off and leave them in peace.

One night as she was seeing him off after a visit with Greta she stepped out onto the steps with him and closed the door so they could talk with some privacy. It was a pleasant evening in early September and not cold.

Staring up at him in the blurred blue of the night, she asked, "Do you never plan to leave us?"

He smiled at her mockingly. "Greta would not want me to go."

"The poor dear is too ill to care much now," Margaret said. "Dr. Grundy says she may die anytime. What then?"

For a change Barnabas showed concern. "She is that ill? I haven't noticed such a drastic change in her."

"Then it must be because you haven't been giving her your attention," Margaret said with some bitterness.

"I care a good deal more for your daughter than you can guess," Barnabas reproved her sharply as they stood together in the darkness. "For a time she was almost a reincarnation of Josette."

"And now it is Judith you see in Josette's role!" she accused him.

Barnabas stiffened. "You have known about that from the beginning."

"I warn you she has no idea of how you feel about her," Margaret said, "of what your intentions are."

"It is up to you to prepare her."

"I have always felt your plan a mistake," Margaret told him. "I can't change my views at this late date."

"Either you tell her or I will," he warned. "I will not lose this chance to rid myself of the curse. I have not watched her grow from childhood into a woman of grace to give her up to someone else."

"Isn't that a matter for her to decide?" Margaret asked.

"If you try to turn her against me you'll regret it," he told her coldly.

"I will say nothing. Judith will be shocked if you suggest her becoming your wife."

"We shall see," he said quietly. And he descended the steps and walked away into the night.

She heard no more on the subject until Judith came to her one evening nearly in tears. Margaret was in her bedroom preparing for dinner. She'd just put on her dress and was arranging her hair when there came a timid knock on the door. When she opened it she saw Judith looking very upset.

"Come in," she told the girl. "What is wrong?"

Judith stared at her in dismay. "I've come from having a talk with Cousin Barnabas and I can't believe what he said."

Margaret was at once alerted. "What did he say?"

The pretty girl crossed in front of her and then turned with an expression of utter incredulity on her face. "He says he wants to marry me!"

"Oh?" Margaret managed a calm exterior.

"It's too preposterous!" Judith went on. "All these years he's been my foster father. I've thought of him as my father. And now he's asking me to marry him."

"What did you tell him?"

Judith frowned. "I was speechless for a moment. Then I told him I wasn't in love with him that way, that I looked upon him as a parent. I pointed out his age and his eccentric way of living—keeping to himself in that old house all day and only coming out at night."

"Did he react to what you said?"

"Yes. He became angry. He said that he was ageless. And if I'd only marry him he'd change his way of life. He would keep ordinary hours and dismiss Hare from his service. We could go to New York or London to live."

"What was your answer to that?"

The blonde sighed. "I told him it was no use. And he asked if I found him repulsive. I told him no. But I did consider both him and his way of life strange. Then he tried to kiss me. And when his lips touched my throat they had a cold, clammy feeling to them that terrified me. It was as if all the strength was draining from me as he kept holding me close. I wanted to scream but I didn't. I knew he'd be hurt. But this chill swept through me as he held me in his arms. Then, at last, he let me go."

Margaret was becoming alarmed and her eyes searched the girl's throat for the telltale marks of red! The marks of the Devil's Kiss, which would eventually make Judith a slave to the will of Barnabas. And she saw them clearly where Barnabas had sunk his teeth into the girl's soft flesh.

"You know you are in great danger," Margaret warned. "He has a strange obsession about you."

"What shall I do?" the girl pleaded.

Margaret placed a comforting arm around her. "You must be strong. And I think you should leave here as soon as possible."

"But I can't do that! Not after all you've done for me! And with Greta still so ill!"

"That doesn't matter," Margaret said. "We must save you. From the moment he adopted you this is what he planned. That you should be his bride."

"But the idea disgusts me!" Judith complained. "And anyway I'm in love with someone else who has asked me to marry him."

This was unexpected. She stared at the girl in amazement. "This is the first I've heard about it."

Judith, now blushing furiously, glanced down. "He is the young man I have had to dinner several times. You and Uncle Jonas liked him."

"The artist?" Margaret questioned, remembering the earnest, dark-haired young painter who Judith had met while he was sketching on the beach.

"Yes," the girl said impulsively. "He is going back to Boston soon. And he wants me to marry him and go with him."

"He seemed very nice," she agreed. "But can he support you? An artist earns so little!"

"Jim's family is very wealthy." Judith told her.

Margaret recalled only that his name was Jim Reeves and he had excellent manners, but she said, "Then I think you should marry this Jim and get away from here as quickly as you can."

"It's too preposterous," Judith went on. "Jim has been planning to ask Cousin Barnabas for permission to marry me. And now this has happened!"

"It won't get better," Margaret warned her. "It will be worse."

"I'll be seeing Jim tonight and I'll talk to him," Judith said. And her face crinkled with dismay. "I hardly know how to begin. It's so embarrassing!"

"You must bring yourself to do it," she insisted. "Before Barnabas becomes angry at your refusal and tries to force you to marry him."

Judith showed alarm. "He wouldn't do that, surely?"

She gave the girl a solemn look. "I'm certain he would." When Judith left her and she lingered to complete her dressing before going downstairs she stared at herself in the mirror. The reflection that she saw was alarming. It shocked her that she had grown so much older and wearier-looking in the past few years. The care and worry over Greta, together with carrying the burden of her knowledge about Barnabas, had taken its toll in the lines marking her once-lovely face and the dark circles under her eyes.

It had cost her dearly to keep her silence concerning the strange man in the old house. In rapid succession she pictured Granny Entwhistle, Patience and Clare Blandish. They had all been victims of Barnabas and his curse. And now it had come to be Judith's turn. Margaret determined she would not fail the lovely child whom she'd raised.

Always she had comforted herself with the idea she could protect Judith when the time came. Well, the time had arrived. And she was no longer so certain of being able to beat the man in the cape.

At dinner she waited until Judith had left the table. While Jonas was lingering over his after-dinner brandy she said, "I believe Judith is seriously interested in that young artist who has been here several times. He has asked her to marry him. And I think she should."

Jonas studied her from under raised eyebrows. He seemed startled. "Judith is a mere child," he protested. "She has lots of time to think about marriage."

"I disagree," Margaret argued. "If she doesn't take this Jim Reeves she may later become involved with someone less desirable. Someone here in the village."

"You sound very sure of that," her husband said with a

frown.

"I happen to know," she said quietly. "I even think Cousin Barnabas is romantically interested in her."

It was another time for Jonas to show astonishment. "Barnabas! Why, he is her foster parent! The idea is indecent!"

"I agree."

"I wish the fellow would go," Jonas fumed on. "Causing gossip in the village with his peculiarities and his liking for barmaids. And Hare doesn't even raise his cap when he passes me!"

"Once Greta is at rest I shall demand that he leave," Margaret said in her easy way. "But he is good for her and while she lives I think he should be allowed to remain."

"You always say that," her husband said, sitting back in his chair. "I rue the day I rented him the old house. And now you tell me he has entertained this disgusting idea of marrying Judith."

"I felt you should understand and see why I favor Jim Reeves."

"I say she shouldn't rush into any marriage," Jonas said testily as he got up from the table. "But then no one ever listens to me."

Margaret sat there a moment after he left and felt better for at least revealing that much of the truth to him. It would give her some chance to turn to him in the crisis she knew was impending.

She saw Jim and Judith meet on the lawn. She was standing in the living room window watching them. And she felt a great relief as they strolled off in the direction of Widow's Hill together. She went in to sit with Greta for a while.

Propped up against several pillows her invalid daughter petulantly asked the time. "Surely Barnabas should be here by now."

"It isn't dusk yet," Margaret reminded her. "He never comes before then."

"And lately he has been staying only a short while," Greta said unhappily. She was terribly thin and just the effort of talking seemed to tire her.

"He knows how ill you are and does not want to tax your strength."

"I wonder," Greta said. "So much of the time he is here he talks about Judith."

"Really?" Margaret was at once on the alert.

"He seems obsessed by her. I know she is young and pretty," Greta went on bitterly, "but I wish he wouldn't talk about her all the time as he does. Last night he asked me if she had any young men friends."

"What did you tell him?"

"I mentioned Jim Reeves, of course," Greta said. "I hoped that would discourage him from going on about her so constanly. I said she might soon be marrying Jim."

Margaret was becoming more uneasy. "What did Cousin Barnabas say to that?"

"He seemed very upset. And he said he would never allow Judith to make a marriage of which he didn't approve. He was her legal guardian."

"I wouldn't tell him anymore about Jim," Margaret warned her. "You'll only be making it harder for Judith and him."

Greta sighed. "I suppose you are right. I do wish you'd go and see if Cousin Barnabas is loitering outside. He sometimes lingers in the garden before coming in. I want to talk to him before I become too tired."

"I'll see," Margaret promised, rising.

But she did not look for him in the garden. Instead she walked out back to the dark, forbidding fagade of the old house. By the time she reached it she caught a glimpse of the tall figure of Barnabas strolling across the field toward her. He was coming from the direction of the family cemetery.

Dusk gave the evening a blurred, eerie light as the gaunt man in the Inverness cape strolled purposefully towards her. She saw that his handsome face was set in a grim expression. He halted directly in front of her.

"I have seen Judith and the young man on Widow's Hill," he began. "I suppose you have encouraged them."

"She was in love with Jim long before you told her how you felt."

His lips worked nervously as he hesitated before replying. Then he said, "I suppose it pleased you that she was revolted by the idea of marrying me."

"I have said nothing to her one way or the other," Margaret insisted.

"I'm afraid I can't believe that," he said coldly. "And I warn you that all this will do you no good. I intend to marry Judith no matter what!"

"She won't have you!"

"We'll see."

"If you try to force her I'll take her down to see you in the daytime," Margaret warned him. "See you as you really are! In your coffin with the lid closed for the daylight hours you cannot face!"

Barnabas grasped her by the arm in a cruel grip. "Don't threaten me!" he warned in a tense voice. "I have too much power to be threatened!"

"You are inhuman! Cruel!" she protested, trying to free herself from his punishing fingers.

"My only chance to be free again is Judith and you'll not stand in my way!"

"That's just a crazy dream of yours," she sobbed. "You are cursed forever! There can't be another Josette! Angelique finished you! She must be laughing at you in her tomb!"

Barnabas uttered a beast-like moan and hurled her to the ground. While she slowly got to her feet he turned and strode swiftly away. He did not pay his usual visit to Greta that night. And the invalid unhappily speculated on his reasons for not doing so as she was being prepared for sleep. Margaret made vague excuses for Barnabas but felt her daughter did not believe them.

Later, when Greta was safely asleep, Margaret went to the front of the house again to watch for Judith. She had no idea where the young lovers had gone after their stroll to Widow's Hill. But she was sure Judith would soon be returning as she never stayed out much later than ten. She moved on into the living room which was in darkness and took up a position at the front window that gave her a full view of the lawn area.

A shaft of moonlight cut in through the window and outlined her figure in the dark. She had the ominous feeling of approaching danger. She had never before fought with Barnabas so openly, and she had never seen him in such a vindictive mood. It could only mean trouble.

Suddenly she saw Jim Reeves and Judith strolling across the lawn in the direction of the house. A short distance from the front door they paused and Jim Reeves took the girl in his arms for a lingering goodnight kiss. Then he walked away while she stood for a moment and waved after him. Margaret felt a deep relief in knowing the girl was safe and would be inside the house in a few seconds.

But her relief quickly turned to terror as Judith approached the front door. Out of the shadows by the door the tall, caped figure of Barnabas emerged. He quickly grasped a hand around Judith's mouth and holding her captive with the other powerful arm he pressed his lips into her neck. Margaret watched the eerie drama of the shadows with frozen horror. She could not move or utter a sound. Then, all at once, the two had vanished.

Breaking the spell, she rushed to the front door and hurled it open but there was no sign of them. The rustling of the bushes in the night wind and the silver emptiness of the moonlit lawn mocked her. She stood there not knowing what to do. Jonas would refuse to believe her. She did not want to bring the servants into it. She was alone and helpless.

She waited in the foyer, sick with despair. The cold moonlight shone in on the portrait of Barnabas and she thought his expression had never been so malevolent. She was staring at the painting with horrified fascination when she heard the faint fumbling at the front door knob. Trembling, she turned as the big door slowly swung open to reveal a dazed-looking Judith standing there.

Margaret rushed to put an arm around her. "Are you all right?"

Judith gave her a vacant, surprised look. "Of course."

"I saw Barnabas approach you. I was terrified!"

The girl stared at her in wonder. "Why should you be? We had a nice walk in the moonlight. He was wonderful to me."

Margaret gasped. There were red marks on the girl's neck, and she recognized the weird, trance-like state into which Judith had fallen. He was using the same hypnotism which had worked so well with Patience and Clare Blandish for a while. He had been right when he'd warned her he had too much power to be threatened.

CHAPTER 13

Dark shadows hovered over Collinwood once again. Margaret knew that Judith was in great danger and yet she could not think of any way to save her. In the beginning she had hoped the girl would run off with the wealthy young artist, Jim Reeves. But that was before Barnabas Collins had used his hypnotic powers on her. Now Judith was well on the way to becoming his slave.

It was fitting that the morning brought a downpour of rain. The weather suited Margaret's somber mood. Nor was her state of mind improved by the alarming deterioration in her invalid daughter's condition. Greta was too weak to sit up for her breakfast. She didn't even want to talk, but lay silently with her eyes closed.

Judith came to join Margaret in the library with a troubled expression on her attractive face. "I've just been in to see Greta," she said. "She seems much worse."

Margaret nodded. "I've sent a note to Dr. Grundy. I hope he'll call before the day is over."

"I think he should get here as soon as possible," Judith worried.

Margaret's eyes sought the girl's throat and she saw the red marks of the Devil's kiss had vanished. And so had Judith's dreamy, preoccupied manner. But from experience she knew it would return again. Barnabas would continue to hypnotize Judith from now on and mercilessly feast on her blood until she was in the same listless dull-eyed state to which he'd reduced Patience and Clare Blandish. By the time the girl was able to shake off the hypnosis she would be a lost soul just as the others had been. Barnabas might hope the alliance would end in a happy marriage to release him from his fate, but Margaret knew better. It was bound to end exactly as before. He would eventually be faced by a rebellious Judith and take out his frustration by throttling her. Margaret knew all this without knowing how to prevent it.

To test the girl's feelings about Barnabas she decided to bring his name into the discussion about the desperately ill Greta. She said, "I think Cousin Barnabas' not calling last night has something to do with Greta's upset."

Judith frowned. "Do his visits mean that much to her?"

"She dotes on Barnabas."

"He is charming," Judith agreed. "And I'm sure if he'd known Greta was so ill he'd have come to see her."

"Perhaps," Margaret said, allowing doubt to show in her tone. "You were with him, weren't you?"

"Yes," Judith agreed with a perplexed look on her pretty face. "It's strange. I can't seem to remember our meeting. But we walked together and he talked about his loneliness. Exactly what he said is vague as well. But it was very pleasant to be with him."

"What about Jim Reeves?" Margaret asked, looking at her very directly.

The blonde girl blushed. "I like Jim."

"And you say he wants to marry you."

"Yes. But I'm frightened. I suddenly have the feeling I shouldn't leave here. That I'm needed at Collinwood." She gave her a wondering look. "Isn't that strange! I've never felt that way before!"

"I think you should fight it," Margaret advised her evenly. "I think you should leave here and marry Jim."

Judith stared at her uncertainly. "I'm so confused. Jim will be going in a few days. He'll want an answer before then."

"If you love him you shouldn't have any trouble making up your mind."

"But I owe so much to all of you," Judith said with a troubled air. "And especially to my foster father, Barnabas."

"Would you be willing to consider his offer of marriage? Do you think you owe him that?" Margaret asked pointedly.

Judith's cheeks showed crimson again. She looked down. "I think that offer was made in desperation. He was afraid of losing me as a daughter. I'd rather not think about it."

"But just yesterday you were frightened and disgusted by the thought of his pressing you to marry him," Margaret went on firmly.

"Why have your feelings changed?"

Judith continued to avoid looking at her. "I don't know," she admitted. "Now I feel only sympathy for him."

"Sympathy can be an expensive luxury," Margaret warned her.

But the hypnosis Barnabas had started on her was already doing its evil work. After a few more sessions it would be impossible to properly reach Judith's mind.

The rain ended in the early afternoon to be replaced by a heavy blanket of fog. View of the ocean and Widow's Hill was shut off from Collinwood. And it even hid the old house which Barnabas had rented. By evening it was prematurely dark. Margaret had spent much of her time with Greta, who had not rallied.

Dr. Grundy arrived just after dinner. Margaret took him to her daughter's bedside. After he had made his first brief examination he accompanied Margaret out of the room to the hallway where they could discuss matters frankly.

The stout doctor looked solemn. "I dislike telling you this, Mrs. Collins, but Greta could be dying."

Pain stirred in Margaret's chest. In a tight voice, she said, "I've been afraid of that."

Dr. Grundy sighed. "Perhaps we should look on it as a welcome release since there is no hope of her recovering. On the other hand, this may only be a serious attack before the final one which will carry her off. She could improve and live on for a few weeks or months. It can't be long."

"I understand, Doctor," Margaret said.

Dr. Grundy drew his large gold watch from a vest pocket and frowned at it. "I have some other calls but I feel I should remain here for a half-hour or so. Just let me be alone with her." He returned the watch to his pocket. "By the way, I brought you a visitor. He came out to see Judith."

Margaret was both surprised and pleased at this news. And when she returned to the living room she found Jim and Judith waiting for her, standing by the fireplace together in a conspiratorial kind of silence. They had the air of having ended a quarrel.

Judith stepped forward. "What does the doctor think about Greta?"

"He thinks she is very ill," Margaret told her. "He's remaining here for a while." She turned to Jim Reeves. "I'm glad you came, Jim."

The tall young man's pleasant face showed a brighter look. "I hope I haven't intruded on your trouble, Mrs. Collins," he said with polite consideration.

"Not at all," she said. "My husband is in the library. The doctor can consult with him at any time. I have a few minutes for you two."

Jim Reeves gave Judith an awkward look and then turned to her again. "Mrs. Collins, I want Judith to leave here with me tomorrow. I'd like her to visit my family in Boston and announce our engagement."

"I think that would be ideal," Margaret said.

"You see!" Jim told the girl reproachfully. "You said Mrs. Collins wouldn't think this was proper. And she does!"

Judith looked unhappy. "I'm not ready for marriage yet, Jim."

"It's that foster father of yours! That Barnabas Collins!" Jim said angrily. "You have been filled with doubts by him! And it's not fair. I say we should talk to him together. Why can't we go visit him at the other house now?"

"He never sees anyone until after dusk," Judith said in a panicky voice.

"It's dark enough for dusk even though it's an hour away," Jim said. "I think we should look him up at once. Let me state my case before both him and you."

Judith gave Margaret an appealing glance. "I think that would be a mistake, don't you?"

Margaret shrugged. "I see no harm in trying to see Cousin Barnabas. Though I doubt if you'll get by Hare." She explained to Jim, "That's his servant. A thoroughly unpleasant character."

"I say let's try," Jim said, taking a reluctant Judith by the arm.

Margaret stood by while Jim helped Judith on with her rain cloak. Then they both went out the front door. She stood alone in the living room, caught between the crisis of her daughter's illness and the one involving Judith and her future. She had little hope the two young people would get inside the gloomy old mansion but she had felt it wrong to discourage them.

She went to a side window to see if she could get a glimpse of them as they made their way through the rear yard. But there was no sign of them. As she stood there staring into the fog a figure gradually took shape amid the swirling wreaths of mist. She strained to make out who it was and suddenly knew it to be Hare!

The burly servant was staggering drunkenly along the path, heading toward the front lawns and the cliff. With fascinated eyes she followed his unsteady progress until the fog swallowed him up again. So the old house had been left unguarded! But would the door be unlocked? She wondered.

Her speculations were brought to an end by the entrance of Dr. Grundy and Jonas. She turned to the two men and saw that her husband looked less tense than before. She took this as a good omen.

Dr. Grundy confirmed her guess. "Your daughter is resting easier. She may pull through this all right. I'll have to get along now."

"Thank you for coming, Doctor," Margaret said, walking with

him to the foyer.

Dr. Grundy paused as he opened the front door allowing the damp air to rush in. "What about the young man? Does he want to return to the village with me?"

"I think not," Margaret said. "We'll have the groom take him in later."

When the doctor had gone Jonas turned to her. "What is that young man doing here tonight?"

"He's leaving tomorrow. He wants Judith to make a decision about their marrying."

Jonas looked pained. "Must that be made a problem at a time like this?"

"There need be no problem," she said quietly. "They've gone to discuss it with Barnabas."

Her husband snorted. "They'll never get near him. He'll give them no hearing since he's after Judith for himself."

"At least they should make an effort to discuss it with him."

"I'll be in the library. I have some important papers to go over," Jonas said. "Ada is with Greta. Let me know if her condition changes. Just now she is sleeping."

Margaret paid a brief visit to the sick room. Her daughter was still resting so she quietly left again. She was on her way down the hall when the front door was thrown open. The moment she saw Jim Reeves and Judith standing framed in the doorway she knew something had happened. Judith wore a stricken expression and Jim was wildly excited.

Judith came running to her. "What does it mean, Aunt Margaret? What awful thing is going on here?"

Margaret halted and stared at her and then at the young man. "Why do you ask that?"

Jim came striding forward. "We got into the old house. Hare left the front door open. It's like a deserted place. Only the living room and a small room at the back being used. We couldn't find Barnabas. There wasn't even a bed in the bedrooms upstairs. We went on down to the cellar." He paused. "There was a doorway opening on a room with a casket in it. There were candles burning on a sideboard. We went close to the casket and we looked in it."

Horror was written on Judith's face as she told her, "And we found Barnabas asleep inside it. Like a dead person. What does it mean?"

"It means he's mad!" Jim said angrily. "And you should not listen to anything he says. You should not even be near him."

"There's more than that to it," Margaret spoke up in a firm voice. "I have tried to spare you this, Judith. But Barnabas is not mad. Neither is he a normal human being."

Judith's eyes widened. "Not a normal human being!"

"He loves you in his own way, so you must not hate him. He has been devoted to you until now. But he bears a curse which dooms him to a life bereft of love. And because of that curse he now presents a danger to you."

Jim Reeves was staring at her with a knowing look. He said, "You call Barnabas Collins not quite normal. And yet you say he is not mentally ill. I think I'm beginning to understand what you mean."

"I doubt that, Jim," she said sadly.

"But I do," he went on with excitement in his tone. "The casket! And his not appearing until dusk! It all fits in! Barnabas has to be a vampire! One of the living dead who feast on human blood! Am I right?"

Margaret did not reply at once. She stood there whitefaced and trembling.

Judith appealed to her. "It can't be anything like that? It's too outlandish!"

"I'm afraid Jim has hit on the secret of Barnabas," she said. "And that is why I want you to leave Collinwood tonight."

Anger and fear shadowed Jim's pleasant face. "She'll leave," he said grimly. "But before we go I want to take care of Barnabas. We haven't much time either. It will be dusk in another ten minutes or so. And before then I must drive a wooden stake through his heart."

Margaret had not expected this. She had hoped he would take Judith away and let it go at that. But a glance at the stern determination of his youthful features and his biting words told her that he intended to kill Barnabas.

She tried to placate him, saying, "It is not your responsibility, Jim!"

"I won't feel Judith's safe until it's done," he told her. And he turned and started for the door.

Judith rushed after him, asking, "Jim, what are you going to do?"

They vanished into the fog-ridden night, leaving the door partly ajar after them. Margaret stared at the open door in consternation realizing what she had done in finally giving Jim Reeves a clue to the truth about Barnabas. Barnabas would be destroyed if Jim had his way. And though it had to be accomplished before dusk, there were still a few remaining minutes for the grisly task.

But what of the desperately ill Greta? A visit from Barnabas might mean the difference between whether she lived or died. She had so come to depend on the gaunt, handsome man. Margaret took only a moment to ponder the predicament. And then she knew she must try to save Barnabas, no matter what. There was no time to waste. She hurried out the door after the other two without waiting to put on a cloak for protection against the cold and damp.

Racing through the yard in the direction of the old house, she could see no sign of the others through the mist. Reaching the front door, she found it open and breathlessly made her way inside and down the narrow cellar stairs. The glow of the candles from the secret room guided her in the darkness and she went in to discover Judith waiting near the entrance with her hands pressed against her cheeks as she stared wide-eyed at Jim. The young artist was standing by the casket with a small garden stake he'd uprooted in one hand and an axe in the other. The tense expression he wore told Margaret that within a moment he would raise the stake and use the blunt edge of the axe to drive it into Barnabas's heart.

Margaret didn't hesitate. She rushed forward to Jim with a warning cry. "Please! Don't!"

The young man turned his shocked white face to her. "It must be done! It's the only way to finish him!"

"No!" she pleaded. "You have to allow him to live!"

"Why?"

"Because of my daughter. Greta is near death at this very moment. He is the only one who may be able to save her. She loves him! And seeing him may cause her to rally!"

Jim Reeves took on a dismayed look. "I have only a moment or so left. There is no time to argue."

"Then leave, as I suggested," Margaret begged. "The groom will let you have a horse and carriage. You can be in Collinsport in time to get the night train to Boston."

The young artist had the stake held high, ready to drive it into the body in the coffin. He frowned. "I'm thinking of Judith."

Now Judith came forward to speak for herself. She took hold of Jim's arm and in a near-hysterical voice, said, "She's right! Do as she says! Let him go on with whatever miserable existence he has. Just get me away from here!"

Jim Reeves sighed. He lowered the stake and let it drop to the floor of the ghostly gray room along with the axe. "Very well," he said with resignation. "We'll go!"

Margaret took Judith in her arms for a hasty kiss. Then she said, "Write to me!"

Judith was in tears. "How can I leave you like this?"

Jim took her roughly by the arm. "There is no time to waste," he said urgently. And he led her out of the secret room.

The two had no sooner vanished in the darkness of the cellar than she heard a faint stirring from the casket behind her. The eerie rustling noise sent a chill of terror through her. Mustering all her courage she turned slowly to see one corpse-like hand grasp a side of the casket and then the other. And with great effort Barnabas raised himself up to a sitting position.

His deep-set eyes burned into hers. "You saved me," he said in a low voice. "Why?"

"You heard. Because of Greta."

Barnabas frowned. "Is she as ill as you said?"

Margaret nodded. "She may be dying."

A strange melancholy flooded across the gaunt, handsome face of the man in the Inverness cape. He stiffly lifted himself over the side of the coffin and in a moment towered over her as he stood by her side.

He stared at her. "So now Judith knows the truth about me! What I am!"

"Yes. It was Jim who guessed," she said, "They're leaving Collinsport. It's for the best. You could never have held her love. It would have ended in disaster as it did with the others."

The face of Barnabas was a stern mask. "How did she find me?" he asked harshly. "How did they get in here and discover me in the casket?"

"Hare," she told him. "He's been drinking again. I saw him a while ago wandering in the direction of the cliffs. He left both the door to the house and the entrance to the secret room open."

Barnabas grasped the silver wolf's head of his cane viciously. "I shall have a word or two to offer Hare."

"Never mind about him," Margaret said. "Please come to the house and be ready to talk to Greta when she wakens. It could mean her life."

He gave her an absent glance. "I'll come to the house shortly," he promised. "First, I have something else to do." And he strode out of the room.

"Not Judith!" she called after him in a panic. "You will let them go!"

But there was no reply from him. She stood there in the weird silence of the stone-walled room. Her eyes came to rest on the wooden stake and the axe where Jim had dropped them. And she began to wonder whether she had been wrong in insisting the artist spare Barnabas.

She left the old house as quickly as she could and hurried back to Collinwood through the foggy darkness. Her teeth chattered from fright and the cold. She was near the breaking point and knew it. She prayed that Judith and her young man had gotten away safely and that Barnabas would not attempt to wreak his vengeance on them.

When she reached the front door of the main house

she found her husband standing there with an impatient angry expression on his broad face. "Where have you been?" he demanded. "Greta is awake and she has been asking for you."

Margaret said, "I had an errand. How is she?"

"Weak," Jonas said in a worried voice. "Too weak for my liking. Come along. She's been waiting long enough." The glow from the single small lamp by Greta's bedside cast a soft light on the invalid girl's face. And Margaret was at once struck by the illusion of beauty it created. Greta looked almost her old self again. And the petulant expression of the seriously ill that had so long been with her seemed to have given away to a placid resignation. Margaret bent over her sick daughter.

From the pillow, Greta looked up at her with a faint smile. "So you have come, Mother."

"Yes. I'm sorry to have been so long," Margaret said.

"I know you are busy," Greta said. "But where is Barnabas? I so want to talk with him."

"He has promised to be here shortly," she told her daughter.

Greta closed her eyes. "Ask him to hurry. I need him by me."

"Perhaps he is outside waiting," Margaret suggested hopefully. "I'll go take a look."

She hurried from the sick room on tiptoe praying that Barnabas might not be far away. She was puzzled by the change in Greta. There was a resignation and beauty about her that had only suddenly shown itself. She hoped that it meant her daughter was going to rally but an inner voice warned her this was not likely.

There was no sign of Barnabas in the foyer. But she noticed there was a light in the living room and she went in through the broad doorway to find him standing alone in the elegant big room studying the portrait of the long-dead Josette which hung above the sideboard.

Hurrying across to him, she said, "I've been looking for you. Greta is awake and asking for you."

Barnabas kept his eyes riveted on the portrait, almost as if he hadn't heard her at all. Then in a quiet voice he spoke, as if to himself. "I made a grave error in placing my hopes on Judith. That was where I went wrong. I shouldn't have turned from your Greta. She is the only one since Josette who has truly loved me. Her love could have saved me!"

Margaret touched his arm. "Perhaps it still can."

Now he turned to her and she had never seen the gaunt face so suffused with sadness. "Let us go to her."

As soon as Greta saw him she lifted a frail hand. "Take my hand in yours, Barnabas," she said. "I've been so lonely without you."

Barnabas took her hand. Margaret winced as she remembered

its cold touch. But it seemed to be welcome to her daughter. Greta smiled. And again Margaret was amazed by the beauty that shone from the emaciated face.

Greta said, "Please don't leave me again, Barnabas. Not ever!"

"I promise," the tall man said solemnly.

There was a dreamy look on the sick girl's face. "It must be a lovely night, Barnabas. With a full moon, the same as those other nights when we went out on the lawn together."

Barnabas rose to the occasion with a gallant lie. "It is a fine, warm evening with a host of stars."

"Let us go out there again! Just for a last moment of happiness," Greta said in a voice that broke slightly.

Barnabas nodded. "A little later, perhaps." And he kept holding her hand in his.

Margaret saw her daughter suddenly go rigid with pain. Her head pressed against the pillow and her back seemed to arch as she raised slightly under the light covering of sheets. Her eyes opened and fixed on Barnabas. Her lips moved but no sound came from them. She quickly went limp and her eyes closed. Barnabas lowered her hand gently to the bed.

Margaret was already beside her daughter, sobbing. "Greta! Greta! Please open your eyes!"

But the eyes did not open and a hasty examination by Jonas brought forth his anguished diagnosis, "She's gone!"

Greta's frail heart had ceased beating at last. Margaret stood at the foot of the bed sobbing as Jonas offered her a comforting arm. In the background the maid, Ada, was crying. Greta lay serenely with the same look of beauty that had illumined her face in the last minutes of her life.

It was Barnabas Collins who made the first move. He had taken Greta's death in stoic fashion. Now he bent down and with a quick gesture gathered the sheets around the limp body and lifted the dead Greta into his arms. Then he carried her lovingly to the door and out.

Jonas started forward as if to stop him. But Margaret restrained her husband and gazing into his shocked face, said, "Let him take her. It can do no harm now."

She had an idea Barnabas would take Greta out into the night. While there were no stars and it was foggy and miserable, he would have at least kept his word to the girl who had truly loved him. But the minutes passed and he did not return.

Margaret began to become alarmed. Jonas took out his grief and perplexity in raging at her. "Why did you allow him to do that mad thing?" he demanded. "You know the man is demented!"

"They loved each other," Margaret said in a low voice.

"Love!" Jonas looked astounded. "Greta never knew what love meant!"

"You are very wrong in that," she reproved him gently. "Her love for Barnabas was full and complete."

"That man will not remain at Collinwood another night!" Jonas fumed. "Cousin or no cousin, I have endured enough from him."

Margaret gave him a look. "I don't think you need worry about that."

And she proved right. They found Greta's body carefully laid out in the tomb beside Josette. Barnabas must have headed straight for the old cemetery when he left the house. Margaret had no opportunity to ask him. She never saw him again. He vanished from Collinsport as though the fog and darkness had swallowed him up for all eternity.

She visited the old house to lock it up after Greta's funeral. And she found that Barnabas had left the door to the hidden room closed. She entered it briefly to be sure the casket was empty. It was. Then she closed it again and made no mention of the room or what it contained to Jonas or anyone else.

Hare was found on the rocks below Widow's Hill, dead. It was plain that he had fallen over the cliff in his drunken state. For a time there was a great deal of gossip about the accident and Barnabas Collins' disappearance. But it was all soon forgotten by everyone but Margaret.

She lived with her memories of those trying days at Collinwood. While she lived she received regular letters from Judith who was happily married to Jim Reeves and living in France. But there was never a word from Barnabas.

Sleet beat on the gravestone bearing the inscription: "Margaret Collins, 1865-1948." And in the howling wind that lashed the isolated cemetery the plaintive feminine voice could be plainly heard: "That was the true story. And it died with me!"

EPILOGUE

Victoria Winters sat before the blazing log fire in the library with Elizabeth Collins. The attractive older woman smiled at her. "All that Grandmother Margaret Collins ever told me about Barnabas' leaving here was that he went shortly after Greta died."

"It's a strange story," Victoria said in awe. "I wonder where he journeyed when he left Collinwood."

"No one seems to have any idea," Elizabeth said. And indicating the journal which Victoria had been reading and which had brought about their discussion, she pointed out, "He never did get in touch with anyone here again."

"What a strange, romantic person he was," Victoria mused, her eyes wandering to the blazing logs. "I suppose he is dead by now."

"I suppose so," Elizabeth agreed. "During World War II one of the young men from here did locate the name of Barnabas Collins in the London phone directory. But when he called on him he was informed by the neighbors that Barnabas had moved somewhere in Scotland because of the blitz."

Victoria speculated. "Perhaps he had a family, even a son with his own name. It could be that another Barnabas Collins might come here one day." She looked at Elizabeth for confirmation.

The older woman sighed. "It could be," she agreed. "Many stranger things have happened at Collinwood." And they both became silent as the storm continued outside.

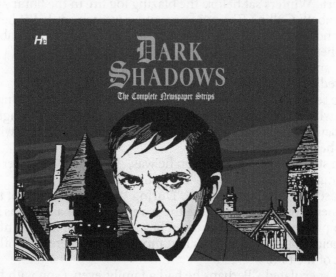